THE HOLLA

BY

Burton Egbert Stevenson

# THE HOLLADAY CASE: A TALE

**Published by Clue Publishing**

**New York City, NY**

**First published circa 1962**

**Copyright © Clue Publishing, 2015**

**All rights reserved**

# ABOUT CLUE PUBLISHING

Everyone loves a classic whodunit, and **Clue Publishing** is devoted to bringing them all to readers, from Sir Arthur Conan Doyle's classic Sherlock Holmes stories to lesser known mysteries written by authors like Richard Marsh and Louis Tracy.

## CHAPTER I: A Bolt from the Blue

The atmosphere of the office that morning was a shade less genial than usual. We had all of us fought our way downtown through such a storm of wind, snow, slush, and sleet as is to be found nowhere save in mid-March New York, and our tempers had suffered accordingly. I had found a cab unobtainable, and there was, of course, the inevitable jam on the Elevated, with the trains many minutes behind the schedule. I was some half-hour late, in consequence, and when I entered the inner office, I was surprised to find Mr. Graham, our senior, already at his desk. He nodded good-morning a little curtly.

"I wish you'd look over these papers in the Hurd case, Lester," he said, and pushed them toward me.

I took them and sat down; and just then the outer door slammed with a violence extremely unusual.

I had never seen Mr. Royce, our junior, so deeply shaken, so visibly distracted, as he was when he burst in upon us a moment later, a newspaper in his hand. Mr. Graham, startled by the noise of his entrance, wheeled around from his desk and stared at him in astonishment.

"Why, upon my word, John," he began, "you look all done up. What's the matter?"

"Matter enough, sir!" and Mr. Royce spread out the paper on the desk before him. "You haven't seen the morning papers, of course; well, look at that!" and he indicated with a trembling finger the article which occupied the first column of the first page—the place of honor.

I saw our senior's face change as he read the headlines, and he seemed positively horror-stricken as he ran rapidly through the story which followed.

"Why, this is the most remarkable thing I ever read!" he burst out at last.

"Remarkable!" cried the other. "Why, it's a damnable outrage, sir! The idea that a gentle, cultured girl like Frances Holladay would deliberately murder her own father—strike him down in cold blood—is too monstrous, too absolutely preposterous, too—too——" and he stopped, fairly choked by his emotion.

The words brought me upright in my chair. Frances Holladay accused of—well!—no wonder our junior was upset!

But Mr. Graham was reading through the article again more carefully, and while he nodded sympathetically to show that he fully assented to the other's words, a straight, deep line of perplexity, which I had come to recognize, formed between his eyebrows.

"Plainly," he said at last, "the whole case hinges on the evidence of this man Rogers—Holladay's confidential clerk—and from what I know of Rogers, I should say that he'd be the last man in the world to make a willful misstatement. He says that Miss Holladay entered her father's office late yesterday afternoon, stayed there ten minutes, and then came out hurriedly. A few minutes later Rogers went into the office and found his employer dead. That's the whole case, but it'll be a hard one to break."

"Well, it must be broken!" retorted the other, pulling himself together with a supreme effort. "Of course, I'll take the case."

"Of course!"

"Miss Holladay probably sent for me last night, but I was out at Babylon, you know, looking up that witness in the Hurd affair. He'll be all right, and his evidence will give us the case. Our answer in the Brown injunction can wait till to-morrow. That's all, I think."

The chief nodded.

"Yes—I see the inquest is to begin at ten o'clock. You haven't much time."

"No—I'd like to have a good man with me," and he glanced in my direction. "Can you spare me Lester?"

My heart gave a jump. It was just the question I was hoping he would ask.

"Why, yes, of course," answered the chief readily. "In a case like this, certainly. Let me hear from you in the course of the day."

Mr. Royce nodded as he started for the door.

"I will; we'll find some flaw in that fellow's story, depend upon it. Come on, Lester."

I snatched up pen and paper and followed him to the elevator. In a moment we were in the street; there were cabs in plenty now, disgorging their loads and starting back uptown again; we hailed one, and in another moment were rattling along toward our destination with such speed as the storm permitted. There were many questions surging through my brain to which I should have welcomed an answer. The storm had cut off my paper that morning, and I regretted now that I had not made a more determined effort to get another. A glance at my companion showed me the folly of attempting to secure any information from his, so I contented myself with reviewing what I already knew of the history of the principals.

I knew Hiram W. Holladay, the murdered man, quite well; not only as every New Yorker knew that multi-millionaire as one of the most successful operators in Wall Street, but personally as well, since he had been a client of Graham & Royce for twenty years and more. He was at that time well on toward seventy years of age, I should say, though he carried his years remarkably well; his wife had been long dead, and he had only one child, his daughter, Frances, who must have been about twenty-five. She had been born abroad, and had spent the first years of her life there with her mother, who had lingered on the Riviera and among the hills of Italy and Switzerland in the hope of regaining a health, which had been failing, so I understood, ever since her daughter's birth. She had come home at last, bringing the black-eyed child with her, and within the year was dead.

Holladay's affections from that moment seemed to grow and center about his daughter, who developed into a tall and beautiful girl—too beautiful, as was soon apparent, for our junior partner's peace of mind. He had met her first in a business way, and afterwards socially, and all of us who had eyes could see how he was eating his heart out at the knowledge that she was far beyond his reach; for it was evident that her father deemed her worthy of a brilliant marriage— as, indeed, she was. I sometimes thought that she held herself at a like value, for though there was about her a constant crowd of suitors, none of them, seemingly, could win an atom of encouragement. She was waiting, I told myself, waiting; and I had even pictured to myself the grim irony of a situation in which our junior might be called upon to arrange her marriage settlements.

The cab stopped with a jolt, and I looked up to see that we had reached the Criminal Courts building. Mr. Royce sprang out, paid the driver, and ran up the steps to the door, I after him. He turned down the corridor to the right, and entered the room at the end of it, which I recognized as the office of Coroner Goldberg. A considerable crowd had already collected there.

"Has the coroner arrived yet?" my companion asked one of the clerks.

"Yes, sir; he's in his private office."

"Will you take him this card and say that I'd like to see him at once, if possible?"

The clerk hurried away with the card. He was back again in a moment.

"This way, sir," he called.

We followed him across the room and through a door at the farther side.

"Ah, Mr. Royce, glad to see you," cried the coroner, as we entered. "We tried to find you last night, but learned that you were out of town, and I was just calling up your office again."

"Miss Holladay asked for me, then?"

"Yes, at once. When we found we couldn't get you, we suggested your senior, but she said she'd wait till you returned."

I could see our junior's face crimson with pleasure.

"You didn't think it necessary to confine her, I trust?" he asked.

"Oh, no; she wasn't disturbed. She spent the night at home—under surveillance."

"That was right. Of course, it's simply absurd to suspect her."

Goldberg looked at him curiously.

"I don't know, Mr. Royce," he said slowly. "If the evidence turns out as I think it will, I shall have to hold her—the district attorney expects it."

Mr. Royce's hands were clutching a chair-back, and they trembled a little at the coroner's words.

"He'll be present at the examination, then?" he asked.

"Yes, we're waiting for him. You see, it's rather an extraordinary case."

"Is it?"

"We think so, anyway!" said the coroner, just a trifle impatiently.

I could see the retort which sprang to our junior's lips, but he choked it back. There was no use offending Goldberg.

"I should like to see Miss Holladay before the examination begins," he said. "Is she present?"

"She's in the next room, yes. You shall see her, certainly, at once. Julius, take Mr. Royce to Miss Holladay," he added to the clerk.

I can see her yet, rising from her chair with face alight, as we entered, and I saw instantly how I had misjudged her. She came a step toward us, holding out her hands impulsively; then, with an effort, controlled herself and clasped them before her.

"Oh, but I'm glad to see you!" she cried in a voice so low I could scarcely hear it. "I've wanted you so much!"

"It was my great misfortune that I could come no sooner," said my chief, his voice trembling a little despite himself. "I—I scarcely expected to see you here with no one——"

"Oh," she interrupted, "there was no one I cared to have. My friends have been very kind—have offered to do anything—but I felt that I wanted to be just alone and think. I should have liked to have my maid, but——"

"She's one of the witnesses, I suppose," explained Mr. Royce. "Well, now that I'm here, I shall stay until I've proved how utterly ridiculous this charge against you is."

She sank back into her chair and looked up at him with dark, appealing eyes.

"You think you can?" she asked.

"Can! Certainly I can! Why, it's too preposterous to stand for a moment! We've only to prove an alibi—to show that you were somewhere else, you know, at the time the crime was committed—and the whole business falls to pieces in an instant. You can do that easily, can't you?"

The color had gone from her cheeks again, and she buried her face in her hands.

"I don't know," she murmured indistinctly. "I must think. Oh, don't let it come to that!"

I was puzzled—confounded. With her good name, her life, perhaps, in the balance, she wanted time to think! I could see that my chief was astonished, too.

"I'll try to keep it from coming to that, since you wish it," he said slowly. "I'll not be able to call you, then, to testify in your own behalf—and that always hurts. But I hope the case will break down at once—I believe it will. At any rate, don't worry. I want you to rely on me."

She looked up at him again, smiling.

"I shall," she murmured softly. "I'm sure I could desire no better champion!"

Well, plainly, if he won this case he would win something else besides. I think even the policeman in the corner saw it, for he turned away with a discretion rare in policemen, and pretended to stare out of the window.

I don't know what my chief would have said—his lips were trembling so he could not speak for the moment—and just then there came a tap at the door, and the coroner's clerk looked in.

"We're ready to begin, sir," he said.

"Very well," cried Mr. Royce. "I'll come at once. Good-by for the moment, Miss Holladay. I repeat, you may rely on me," and he hastened from the room as confidently as though she had girded him for the battle. Instead, I told myself, she had bound him hand and foot before casting him down into the arena.

## CHAPTER II: In the Grip of Circumstance

The outer room was crowded from end to end, and the atmosphere reeked with unpleasant dampness. Only behind the little railing before the coroner's desk was there breathing space, and we sank into our seats at the table there with a sigh of relief.

One never realizes how many newspapers there are in New York until one attends an important criminal case—that brings their people out in droves and swarms. The reporters took up most of the space in this small room, paper and pencils were everywhere in evidence, and in one corner there was a man with a camera stationed, determined, I suppose, to get a photograph of our client, should she be called to the stand, since none could be obtained in any other way.

I saw Singleton, the district attorney, come in and sit down near the coroner, and then the jury filed in from their room and took their seats. I examined them, man by man, with some little anxiety, but they all seemed intelligent and fairly well-to-do. Mr. Royce was looking over their names, and he checked them off carefully as the clerk called the roll. Then he handed the list up to the coroner with a little nod.

"Go ahead," he said. "They're all right, I guess—they look all right."

"It's a good jury," replied the coroner, as he took the paper. "Better than usual. Are you ready, Mr. Singleton?"

"Yes," said the district attorney. "Oh, wait a minute," he added, and he got up and came down to our table. "You're going to put Miss Holladay on the stand, I suppose——"

"And expose her to all this?" and our junior looked around the room. "Not if I can help it!"

"I don't see how you can help it. An alibi's the only thing that can save her from being bound over."

"We'll cross that bridge when we come to it," retorted Mr. Royce. "I think the case against her will soon die of inanition."

"Oh, very well," and Singleton abruptly went back to his desk, biting his mustache thoughtfully. He had made something of a reputation, since his election a year before, as a solver of abstruse criminal problems, and had secured a conviction in two or three capital cases which had threatened for a time to baffle the police. He evidently scented something of the same kind here, or he would have entrusted the case to one of his assistants. It might be added that, while his successes had made him immensely popular with the multitude, there had been, about one or two of them, a hint of unprofessional conduct, which had made his brethren of the bar look rather askance at him.

He nodded to the coroner after a moment, the room was called to order, and the first witness summoned.

It was Rogers, the confidential clerk. I knew Rogers, of course, had talked with him often in a business way, and had the highest respect for him. He had been with Mr. Holladay much longer than I had been with Graham & Royce, and had, as Mr. Graham had pointed out, an unimpeachable reputation.

There were the usual preliminaries, name, age, residence, and so on, Coroner Goldberg asking the questions. He was a really good cross-examiner, and soon came to the core of the matter.

"What is the position of your desk in Mr. Holladay's office?" he asked.

"There is an outer office for the clerks; opening from that, a smaller room where my desk is placed. Opening from my room was Mr. Holladay's private office.

"Had Mr. Holladay's office any other door?"

"No, sir."

"Could entrance be had by the windows?"

"The windows open on the street side of the building. We occupy a part of the eighth floor."

"The fire-escapes——"

"Are at the back of the building—there are none on the street side—nothing but a sheer wall."

"So that anyone entering or leaving the private office must necessarily pass by your desk?"

"Necessarily; yes, sir."

"Could anyone pass without your seeing him?"

"No, sir; that would be quite impossible."

The coroner leaned back in his chair. There was one point settled.

"Now, Mr. Rogers," he said, "will you kindly tell us, in your own way and with as much detail as possible, exactly what happened at your office shortly before five o'clock yesterday afternoon?"

I could see that Rogers was deeply moved. His face was very white, he moistened his lips nervously from time to time, and his hands grasped convulsively the arms of his chair. Plainly, the task before him was far from an agreeable one.

"Well, sir," he began, "we had a very busy day yesterday, and were at the office considerably later than usual; but by five o'clock we had closed up work for the day, and all the other clerks, with the exception of the office-boy, had gone home. I had made some notes from Mr. Holladay's dictation, and had returned to my desk to arrange them, when the outer door opened and Mr. Holladay's daughter came in. She asked me whether her father was engaged, and upon my saying no, opened the inner door and entered his office. She remained, I should think, about ten minutes; then she came out again, walked rapidly past without looking at me, and, I suppose, left the building. I finished arranging my notes, and then entered Mr. Holladay's office to ask if he had any further instructions for me, and I found him lying forward on his desk, with a knife sticking in his neck and the blood spurting out. I summoned aid, but he died without regaining consciousness—I should say he was practically dead when I found him."

I felt, rather than heard, the little stir which ran through the room. There was an indefinable horror in the story and in the conclusion to which it inevitably led.

"Now, let us go back a moment," said the coroner, as Rogers stopped and mopped his forehead feverishly. "I want the jury to understand your story thoroughly. Mr. Holladay had been dictating to you?"

"Yes."

"And was quite well?"

"Yes—as well as usual. He'd been suffering with indigestion for some time past."

"Still he was able to attend to business?"

"Oh, yes, sir. There was nothing at all serious in his illness."

"You then left his office and returned to your own. How long had you been there before the outer door opened?"

"Not over five minutes."

"And who was it entered?"

"Miss Frances Holladay—the daughter of my employer."

"You're quite sure? You know her well?"

"Very well. I've known her for many years. She often drove to the office in the evening to take her father home. I supposed that was what she came for yesterday."

"You looked at her attentively?"

Rogers hitched impatiently in his chair.

"I glanced at her, as I always do," he said. "I didn't stare."

"But you're quite sure it was Miss Holladay?"

"Absolutely sure, sir. Good God!" he cried, his nerves giving way for an instant, "do you suppose I'd make an assertion like that if I wasn't absolutely sure?"

"No," said the coroner soothingly; "no, I don't suppose any such thing, not for a moment, Mr. Rogers; only I want the jury to see how certain the identification is. Shall I proceed?"

"Go ahead, sir," said Rogers. "I'll try to hold myself together a little better, sir."

"I can see what a strain this is for you," said the coroner kindly; "and I'll spare you as much as I can. Now, after Miss Holladay entered the inner office, how long did she remain there?"

"About ten minutes, I should say; not longer than that, certainly."

"Did you hear any sound of conversation, or any unusual noise of any kind?"

"No, sir. It would have been a very unusual noise to be audible. Mr. Holladay's office has heavy walls and a double door which completely shut off all sounds from within."

"Miss Holladay then came out?"

"Yes, sir."

"And walked past you?"

"Yes, sir; walked past me rapidly."

"Did you not think that peculiar?"

"Why, sir, she didn't often stop to speak to me. I was busy and so thought nothing particularly about it."

"Did you notice her face? Did she seem perturbed?"

"No, sir; I didn't notice. I just glanced up and bowed. In fact, I didn't see her face at all, for she had lowered her veil."

"Her veil!" repeated the coroner. "You hadn't mentioned that she wore a veil."

"No, sir; when she came into the office she had lifted it up over her hat-brim—you know how women do."

"Yes—so you saw her face distinctly when she entered?"

"Yes, sir."

"But when she went out, she had lowered her veil. Was it a heavy one?"

"Why, sir," the witness hesitated, "just an ordinary veil, I should say."

"But still heavy enough to conceal her face?"

"Oh, yes, sir."

The coroner nodded. "Now, Mr. Rogers, how long a time elapsed after the departure of the woman before you went back into the inner office?"

"Not more than three or four minutes. I thought perhaps Mr. Holladay was getting ready to accompany his daughter, and I didn't wish to detain him."

"And you found him, as you say, lying forward across his desk with a knife in his throat and the blood spurting out. Did you recognize the knife?"

"Yes, sir. It was his knife—a knife he kept lying on his desk to sharpen pencils with and erase and so on."

"Sharp, was it?"

"It had one long blade, very sharp, sir."

The coroner picked up a knife that was lying on the desk before him.

"Is this the knife?" he asked.

Rogers looked at it carefully.

"That's the knife, sir," he said, and it was passed to the jury. When they had finished with it, Mr. Royce and I examined it. It was an ordinary one-bladed erasing knife with ivory handle. It was open, the blade being about two inches and a half in length, and, as I soon convinced myself, very sharp indeed.

"Will you describe Mr. Holladay's position?" continued the coroner.

"He was lying forward on the desk, with his arms outstretched and his head to one side."

"And there was a great deal of blood?"

"Oh, a great deal! Someone, apparently, had attempted to check it, for a little distance away there was a handkerchief soaked in blood."

The coroner picked up a handkerchief and handed it to the witness.

"Is that the handkerchief?" he asked.

"Yes, sir," said Rogers, after a moment.

"Is it a man's or a woman's handkerchief?"

"Oh, a woman's undoubtedly."

The jury examined it and so did we. It was a small square of fine cambric with no mark that I could see, soaked through and through with blood—unquestionably a woman's handkerchief. Then Rogers told the rest of the story—how he had summoned aid and informed the police.

"Now, Mr. Rogers," said the coroner, when he had finished, "there is one point more. Has there been anything in your knowledge of Mr. Holladay or his business to suggest the idea of suicide?"

The witness shook his head decidedly.

"Nothing whatever, sir," he said positively. "His business was prospering; he was happy and contented—why, he was planning for a trip abroad with his daughter."

"Let us suppose for a moment," continued Goldberg, "that he did actually stab himself in his daughter's presence; what would you naturally expect her to do?"

"I should expect her to give the alarm—to summon aid," replied Rogers.

"Certainly—unquestionably," and Goldberg nodded to my chief. "I turn the witness over to you, Mr. Royce," he said.

"Now, Mr. Rogers," began our junior impressively, "you know, of course, that this whole case hinges, at present, on your identification of the woman who, presumably, was in Mr. Holladay's office when he was stabbed. I want to be very sure of that identification. Will you tell me how she was dressed?"

The witness paused for a moment's thought.

"She wore a dress of very dark red," he said at last, "with some sort of narrow dark trimming—black, possibly. That's all I can tell you about it."

"And the hat?"

"I didn't notice the hat, sir. I only glanced at her."

"But in that glance, Mr. Rogers, did you see nothing unusual—nothing which suggested to your mind that possibly it might not be Miss Holladay?"

"Nothing, sir."

"Some change of demeanor, perhaps; of expression?"

The witness hesitated.

"I thought she was looking not quite so well as usual," he said slowly. "She seemed a little pale and worried."

"Ah! It was dark in the office, was it not, at five o'clock yesterday afternoon?"

"We had turned on the lights half an hour before, sir."

"Is your office well lighted?"

"I have a light over my desk, sir, and there's another on the wall."

"So you could not see your visitor's face with absolute clearness?"

"No, sir; but quite clearly enough to recognize her," he added doggedly.

"Yet you thought her looking pale and worried."

"Yes, sir; that was my impression."

"And when she asked for Mr. Holladay, did she use the words 'my father,' as your evidence would suggest?"

Again the witness hesitated in the effort at recollection.

"No, sir," he answered finally. "Her words, I think, were, 'Is Mr. Holladay engaged at present?'"

"It was Miss Holladay's voice?"

"I could not say, sir," answered the witness, again mopping the perspiration from his forehead. "I have no wish to incriminate Miss Holladay unnecessarily. I'm not sufficiently well acquainted with her voice to swear to it."

"Well, when you answered her question in the negative, did she hesitate before entering the private office?"

"No, sir; she went straight to it."

"Is there any lettering on the door?"

"Oh, yes, the usual lettering, 'Private Office.'"

"So that, even if she were not acquainted with the place, she might still have seen where to go?"

"Yes, sir; I suppose so."

"And you stated, too, I believe, that you could have heard no sound of an altercation in the private office, had one occurred?"

"No, sir; I could have heard nothing."

"You have been with Mr. Holladay a long time, I believe, Mr. Rogers?"

"Over thirty years, sir."

"And you are intimately acquainted with his affairs?"

"Yes, sir."

"Now, Mr. Rogers, have you ever, in all these years, ran across anything—any item of expenditure, any correspondence, anything whatever—which would lead you to think that Mr. Holladay was a victim of blackmail, or that he had ever had a liaison with a woman?"

"No, sir!" cried the witness. "No, sir! I'm willing to swear that such a thing is not possible. I should inevitably have found it out had it existed."

"That will do for the present," said Mr. Royce. "I shall want to recall the witness, however, sir."

The coroner nodded, and Rogers stepped down, still trembling from the effects of his last outburst. I confess that, for my part, I thought we were very deep in the mire.

The office-boy was called next, but added nothing to the story. He had gone to the chute to mail some letters; the woman must have entered the office while he was away. He saw her come out again, but, of course, did not see her face. He had been employed recently, and did not know Miss Holladay.

Then the physicians who had attended the dead man were called, and testified that the knife-blade had penetrated the left carotid artery, and that he had bled to death—was dead, indeed, before they reached him. It would take, perhaps, ten minutes to produce such an effusion of blood as Rogers had noticed—certainly more than five, so that the blow must have been struck before the woman left the inner office.

The policeman who had responded to the alarm testified that he had examined the windows, and that they were both bolted on the inside, precluding the possibility of anyone swinging down from above or clambering up from below. Nothing in the office had been disturbed. There was other evidence of an immaterial nature, and then Miss Holladay's maid was called.

"Was your mistress away from home yesterday afternoon?" asked the coroner.

"Yes, sir; she had the carriage ordered for three o'clock. She was driven away shortly after that."

"And what time did she return?"

"About six, sir; just in time to dress for dinner."

"Did you notice anything unusual in her demeanor when she returned?"

The maid hesitated, fearing doubtless that she might say too much.

"Miss Holladay had complained of a headache in the morning," she said, after a moment. "She was looking badly when she went out, and the drive made her worse instead of better. She seemed very nervous and ill. I advised her to lie down and not dress for dinner, but she would not listen. She always dined with her father, and did not wish to disappoint him. She was in a great hurry, fearing that he'd get back before she was ready."

"There's no doubt in your mind that she was really expecting him?"

"Oh, no, sir; she even went to the door to look for him when he did not come. She seemed very uneasy about him."

That was one point in our favor certainly.

"And when the news of her father's death reached her, how did she bear it?"

"She didn't bear it at all, sir," answered the maid, catching her breath to choke back a sob. "She fainted dead away. Afterwards, she seemed to be in a kind of daze till the doctor came."

"That is all. Have you any questions to ask the witness, Mr. Royce?"

"Only one," said my chief, leaning forward. I knew what it was, and held my breath, wondering whether it were wise to ask it. "Do you remember the gown your mistress wore yesterday afternoon?" he questioned.

"Oh, yes, sir," and the witness brightened. "It was a dark red broadcloth, made very plain, with only a little narrow black braid for trimming."

## CHAPTER III: The Coil Tightens

From the breathless silence that followed her answer, she saw that she had somehow dealt her mistress a heavy blow, and the sobs burst out beyond control, choking her. I could see how my chief's face turned livid. He had driven another rivet in the chain—just the one it needed to hold it firmly together. My head was whirling. Could it be possible, after all, that this gentle, cultured girl was really such a fiend at heart that she could strike down.... I put the thought from me. It was monstrous, unbelievable!

The coroner and the district attorney were whispering together, and I saw the former glance from the blood-stained handkerchief on the desk before him to the sobbing woman on the stand. It needed only that—her identification of that square of cambric—to complete the evidence. He hesitated a moment, said another word or two to Singleton, then straightened up again in his chair. Perhaps he thought the chain was strong enough; perhaps he saw only that the witness was in no condition to go on.

"Anything further, Mr. Royce?" he asked.

"Not at present, sir," answered our junior hoarsely. I think he was just beginning fully to realize how desperate our case was.

"We will dismiss the witness, then, temporarily," said the coroner. "We shall probably recall her later on."

The maid was led back to the witness room on the verge of hysteria, and Goldberg looked over the papers on his desk.

"We have one more witness," he said at last, "Miss Holladay's coachman, and perhaps a little testimony in rebuttal. If you wish to adjourn for lunch, Mr. Royce, I'm quite ready to do so."

"Thank you, sir," said my chief, welcoming any opportunity to pull himself together and prepare a plan of defense. "I do wish it."

"Very well, then; we'll adjourn till two o'clock," and he pushed back his chair.

"May I have one word with you, sir?" asked Mr. Royce.

"Certainly."

"I should like to see Miss Holladay a few moments in private. We wish, of course, to arrange our rebuttal."

The coroner looked at him for a moment with eyes in which just a tinge of curiosity flickered.

"I'll be very glad to allow you to see her in private," he answered readily. "I regret greatly that we couldn't find you last night, so that you could have opportunity to prepare for this hearing. I feel that, in a way, we haven't been quite fair to you, though I don't see how delay could have altered matters, and, in a case of this kind, prompt action is important. I had no intention of placing Miss Holladay on the witness stand, so I thought it best to proceed at once with the inquest. You must admit, sir, that, as the case stands, there's only one course open to me."

"I fear so," assented the other sadly. "It's a most incomprehensible case. The chain of evidence seems absolutely complete, and yet I'm convinced—as every sane man must be—that there is in it some fatal flaw, which, once discovered, will send the whole structure tottering. It must be my business to find that flaw."

"Strange things happen in this world, Mr. Royce," observed Singleton with a philosophy born of experience.

"The impossible never happens, sir!" retorted our junior. "I hope to show you that this belongs in that category."

"Well, I hope you will," said the district attorney. "I'd be glad to find that someone else is guilty."

"I'll do my best," and Mr. Royce turned to me. "Lester, you'd better go and get some lunch. You look quite done up."

"Shall I bring you something?" I asked. "Or, better still, have a meal ready for you in half an hour? Rotin's is just around the corner."

He would have refused, I think, had not the coroner interfered.

"You'd better go, Mr. Royce," he said. "You're looking done up yourself. Perhaps you can persuade Miss Holladay to eat something. I'm sure she needs it."

"Very well, then; have two meals ready in half an hour, Lester," he said, "and a lunch we can bring back with us. I'll go to Miss Holladay now, and then come direct to Rotin's."

He hurried away after the coroner, and I walked slowly over to Rotin's to give the necessary orders. I chose a table in a snug corner, picked up a paper, and tried to read. Its one great item of news was the Holladay case, and I grew hot with anger, as I saw how unquestioningly, how complacently, it accepted the theory of the daughter's guilt. Still, I asked myself, was it to blame? Was anyone to blame for thinking her guilty after hearing the evidence? How could one escape it? Why, even I——

Preposterous! I tried to reason calmly; to find an opening in the net. Yet, how complete it was! The only point we had gained, so far, was that the mysterious visitor had asked for Mr. Holladay, not for her father—and what an infinitesimal point it was! Supposing there had been a quarrel, an estrangement, would not she naturally have used those very words? After all, did not the black eyes, the full lips, the deep-colored cheeks bespeak a strong and virile temperament, depth of emotion, capacity for swift and violent anger? But what cause could there be for a quarrel so bitter, so fierce, that it should lead to such a tragedy? What cause? And then, suddenly, a wave of light broke in upon me. There could be only one—yes, but there could be one! Capacity for emotion meant capacity for passion. If she had a lover, if she had clung to him despite her father! I knew his reputation for severity, for cold and relentless condemnation. Here was an explanation, certainly!

And then I shook myself together angrily. Here was I, reasoning along the theory of her guilt—trying to find a motive for it! I remembered her as I had seen her often, driving with her father; I recalled the many stories I had heard of their devotion; I reflected how her whole life, so far as I knew it, pointed to a nature singularly calm and self-controlled, charitable and loving. As to the lover theory, did not the light in her eyes which had greeted our junior disprove that, at once and forever? Certainly, there was some fatal flaw in the evidence, and it was for us to find it.

I leaned my head back against the wall with a little sigh of relief. What a fool I had been! Of course, we should find it! Mr. Royce had spoken the words, the district attorney had pointed out the way. We had only to prove an alibi! And the next witness would do it. Her coachman had only to tell where he had driven her, at what places she had stopped, and the whole question would be settled. At the hour the crime was committed, she had doubtless been miles away from Wall Street! So the question would be settled—settled, too, without the necessity of Miss Holladay undergoing the unpleasant ordeal of cross-examination.

"It is a most extraor-rdinary affair," said a voice at my elbow, and I turned with a start to see that the chair just behind me had been taken by a man who was also reading an account of the crime. He laid the paper down, and caught my eye. "A most extraor-rdinary affair!" he repeated, appealing to me.

I nodded, merely glancing at him, too preoccupied to notice him closely. I got an impression of a florid face, of a stout, well-dressed body, of an air unmistakably French.

"You will pardon me, sir," he added, leaning a little forward. "As a stranger in this country, I am much inter-rested in your processes of law. This morning I was present at the trial—I per-rceived you there. It seemed to me that the young lady was in—what you call—a tight place."

He spoke English very well, with an accent of the slightest. I glanced at him again, and saw that his eyes were very bright and that they were fixed upon me intently.

"It does seem so," I admitted, loth to talk, yet not wishing to be discourteous.

"The ver' thing I said to myself!" he continued eagerly. "The—what you call—coe-encidence of the dress, now!"

I did not answer; I was in no humor to discuss the case.

"You will pardon me," he repeated persuasively, still leaning forward, "but concer-rning one point I should like much to know. If she is thought guilty what will occur?"

"She will be bound over to the grand jury," I explained.

"That is, she will be placed in prison?"

"Of course."

"But, as I understand your law, she may be released by bondsmen."

"Not in a capital case," I said; "not in a case of this kind, where the penalty may be death."

"Ah, I see," and he nodded slowly. "She would then not be again released until after she shall have been proved innocent. How great a time would that occupy?"

"I can't say—six months—a year, perhaps."

"Ah, I see," he said again, and drained a glass of absinthe he had been toying with. "Thank you, ver' much, sir."

He arose and went slowly out, and I noted the strength of his figure, the short neck——

The waiter came with bread and butter, and I realized suddenly that it was long past the half-hour. Indeed, a glance at my watch showed me that nearly an hour had gone. I waited fifteen minutes longer, ate what I could, and, taking a box-lunch under my arm, hurried back to the coroner's office. As I entered it, I saw a bowed figure sitting at the table, and my heart fell as I recognized our junior. His whole attitude expressed a despair absolute, past redemption.

"I've brought your lunch, Mr. Royce," I said, with what lightness I could muster. "The proceedings will commence in half an hour—you'd better eat something," and I opened the box.

He looked at it for a moment, and then began mechanically to eat.

"You look regularly done up," I ventured. "Wouldn't I better get you a glass of brandy? That'll tone you up."

"All right," he assented listlessly, and I hurried away on the errand.

The brandy brought a little color back to his cheeks, and he began to eat with more interest.

"Must I order lunch for Miss Holladay?" I questioned.

"No," he said. "She said she didn't wish any."

He relapsed again into silence. Plainly, he had received some new blow during my absence.

"After all," I began, "you know we've only to prove an alibi to knock to pieces this whole house of cards."

"Yes, that's all," he agreed. "But suppose we can't do it, Lester?"

"Can't do it?" I faltered. "Do you mean——?"

"I mean that Miss Holladay positively refuses to say where she spent yesterday afternoon."

"Does she understand the—the necessity?" I asked.

"I pointed it out to her as clearly as I could. I'm all at sea, Lester."

Well, if even he were beginning to doubt, matters were indeed serious!

"It's incomprehensible!" I sighed, after a moment's confused thought. "It's——"

"Yes—past believing."

"But the coachman——"

"The coachman's evidence, I fear, won't help us much—rather the reverse."

I actually gasped for breath—I felt like a drowning man from whose grasp the saving rope had suddenly, unaccountably, been snatched.

"In that case——" I began, and stopped.

"Well, in that case?"

"We must find some other way out," I concluded lamely.

"Is there another way, Lester?" he demanded, wheeling round upon me fiercely. "Is there another way? If there is, I wish to God you'd show it to me!"

"There must be!" I protested desperately, striving to convince myself. "There must be; only, I fear, it will take some little time to find."

"And meanwhile, Miss Holladay will be remanded! Think what that will mean to her, Lester!"

I had thought. I was desperate as he—but to find the flaw, the weak spot in the chain, required, I felt, a better brain than mine. I was lost in a whirlwind of perplexities.

"Well, we must do our best," he went on more calmly, after a moment. "I haven't lost hope yet—chance often directs these things. Besides, at worst, I think Miss Holladay will change her mind. Whatever her secret, it were better to reveal it than to spend a single hour in the Tombs. She simply must change her mind! And thanks, Lester, for your thoughtfulness. You've put new life into me."

I cleared away the débris of the lunch, and a few moments later the room began to fill again. At last the coroner and district attorney came in together, and the former rapped for order.

"The inquest will continue," he said, "with the examination of John Brooks, Miss Holladay's coachman."

I can give his evidence in two words. His mistress had driven directly down the avenue to Washington Square. There she had left the carriage, bidding him wait for her, and had continued southward into the squalid French quarter. He had lost sight of her in a moment, and had driven slowly about for more than two hours before she reappeared. She had ordered him to drive home as rapidly as he could, and he had not stopped until he reached the house. Her gown? Yes, he had noticed that it was a dark red. He had not seen her face, for it was veiled. No, he had never before driven her to that locality.

Quaking at heart, I realized that only one person could extricate Frances Holladay from the coil woven about her. If she persisted in silence, there was no hope for her. But that she should still refuse to speak was inconceivable, unless——

"That is all," said the coroner. "Will you cross-examine the witness, Mr. Royce?"

My chief shook his head silently, and Brooks left the stand.

Again the coroner and Singleton whispered together.

"We will recall Miss Holladay's maid," said the former at last.

She was on the stand again in a moment, calmer than she had been, but deadly pale.

"Are your mistress's handkerchiefs marked in any way?" Goldberg asked, as she turned to him.

"Some of them are, yes, sir, with her initials, in the form of a monogram. Most of them are plain."

"Do you recognize this one?" and he handed her the ghastly piece of evidence.

I held my breath while the woman looked it over, turning it with trembling fingers.

"No, sir!" she replied emphatically, as she returned it to him.

"Does your mistress possess any handkerchiefs that resemble this one?"

"Oh, yes, sir; it's an ordinary cambric handkerchief of good quality such as most ladies use."

I breathed a long sigh of relief; here, at least, fortune favored us.

"That is all. Have you any questions, Mr. Royce?"

Again our junior shook his head.

"That concludes our case," added the coroner. "Have you any witnesses to summon, sir?"

What witnesses could we have? Only one—and I fancied that the jurymen were looking at us expectantly. If our client were indeed innocent, why should we hesitate to put her on the stand, to give her opportunity to defend herself, to enable her to shatter, in a few words, this chain of circumstance so firmly forged about her? If she were innocent, would she not naturally wish to speak in her own behalf? Did not her very unwillingness to speak argue——

"Ask for a recess," I whispered. "Go to Miss Holladay, and tell her that unless she speaks——"

But before Mr. Royce could answer, a policeman pushed his way forward from the rear of the room and handed a note to the coroner.

"A messenger brought this a moment ago, sir," he explained.

The coroner glanced at the superscription and handed it to my chief.

"It's for you, Mr. Royce," he said.

I saw that the address read,

For Mr. Royce,

Attorney for the Defense.

He tore it open, and ran his eyes rapidly over the inclosure. He read it through a second time, then held out the paper to me with an expression of the blankest amazement. The note read:

The man Rogers is lying. The woman who was with Holladay wore a gown of dark green.

## CHAPTER IV: I Have an Inspiration

I stared at the lines in dumb bewilderment. "The man Rogers is lying." But what conceivable motive could he have for lying? Besides, as I looked at him on the stand, I would have sworn that he was telling the truth, and very much against his will. I had always rather prided myself upon my judgment of human nature—had I erred so egregiously in this instance? "The woman who was with Holladay wore a gown of dark green." Who was the writer of the note? How did he know the color of her gown? There was only one possible way he could know—he knew the woman. Plainly, too, he must have been present at the morning hearing. But if he knew so much, why did he not himself come forward? To this, too, there was but one answer—he must be an accomplice. But then, again, if he were an accomplice, why should he imperil himself by writing this note, for it could very probably be traced? I found myself deeper in the mire, farther from the light, at every step.

"Do you wish to summon any witnesses, Mr. Royce?" asked the coroner again. "I shall be glad to adjourn the hearing until to-morrow if you do."

Mr. Royce roused himself with an effort.

"Thank you, sir," he said. "I may ask you to do that later on. Just at present, I wish to recall Mr. Rogers."

"Very well," said the coroner, and Rogers was summoned from the witness room.

I looked at him attentively, trying to fathom his thoughts, to read behind his eyes; but look as I might, I could see nothing in his face save concern and grief. He had grown gray in Holladay's office; he had proved himself, a hundred times, a man to be relied on; he had every reason to feel affection and gratitude toward his employer, and I was certain that he felt both; he received a liberal salary, I knew, and was comfortably well-to-do.

That he himself could have committed the crime or been concerned in it in any way was absolutely unthinkable. Yet why should he lie? Above all, why should he seek to implicate his employer's daughter? Even if he wished to implicate her, how could he have known the color of her gown? What dark, intricate problem was this that confronted us?

In the moment that followed, I saw that Mr. Royce was studying him, too, was straining to find a ray of light for guidance. If we failed now——

I read the note through again—"a gown of dark green"—and suddenly, by a kind of clairvoyance, the solution of the mystery leaped forth from it. I leaned over to my chief, trembling with eagerness.

"Mr. Royce," I whispered hoarsely, "I believe I've solved the puzzle. Hold Rogers on the stand a few moments until I get back."

He looked up at me astonished; then nodded, as I seized my hat, and pushed my way through the crowd. Once outside the building, I ran to the nearest dry-goods house—three blocks away it was, and what fearfully long blocks they seemed!—then back again to the courtroom. Rogers was still on the stand, but a glance at Mr. Royce told me that he had elicited nothing new.

"You take him, Lester," he said, as I sat down beside him. "I'm worn out."

Quivering with apprehension, I arose. It was the first time I had been given the center of the stage in so important a case. Here was my opportunity! Suppose my theory should break down, after all!

"Mr. Rogers," I began, "you've been having some trouble with your eyes, haven't you?"

He looked at me in surprise.

"Why, yes, a little," he said. "Nothing to amount to anything. How did you know?"

My confidence had come back again. I was on the right track, then!

"I did not know," I said, smiling for the first time since I had entered the room. "But I suspected. I have here a number of pieces of cloth of different colors. I should like you to pick out the one that most nearly approximates the color of the gown your visitor wore yesterday afternoon."

I handed him the bundle of samples, and as I did so, I saw the district attorney lean forward over his desk with attentive face. The witness looked through the samples slowly, while I watched him with feverish eagerness. Mr. Royce had caught an inkling of my meaning and was watching him, too.

"There's nothing here," said Rogers, at last, "which seems quite the shade. But this is very near it."

He held up one of the pieces. With leaping heart, I heard the gasp of astonishment which ran around the room. The jurymen were leaning forward in their chairs.

"And what is the color of that piece?" I asked.

"Why, dark red. I've stated that already."

I glanced triumphantly at the coroner.

"Your honor," I said, as calmly as I could, "I think we've found the flaw in the chain. Mr. Rogers is evidently color-blind. As you see, the piece he has selected is a dark green."

The whole audience seemed to draw a deep breath, and a little clatter of applause ran around the room. I could hear the scratch, scratch of the reporters' pencils—here was a situation after their hearts' desire! Mr. Royce had me by the hand, and was whispering brokenly in my ear.

"My dear fellow; you're the best of us all; I'll never forget it!"

But Rogers was staring in amazement from me to the cloth in his hand, and back again.

"Green!" he stammered. "Color-blind! Why, that's nonsense! I've never suspected it!"

"That's probable enough," I assented. "The failing is no doubt a recent one. Most color-blind persons don't know it until their sight is tested. Of course, we shall have an oculist examine you; but I think this evidence is pretty conclusive."

Coroner Goldberg nodded, and the district attorney settled back in his chair.

"We've no further questions to ask this witness at present," I continued. "Only I'd like you to preserve this piece of cloth, sir," and I handed it to Goldberg. He placed it with the other exhibits on his desk, and I sat down again beside my chief. He had regained all his old-time energy and keenness—he seemed another man.

"I should like to recall Miss Holladay's maid, if you please," he said; and the girl was summoned, while Rogers stumbled dazedly off to the witness room.

"You're quite sure your mistress wore a dark red gown yesterday afternoon?" he asked, when the girl was on the stand again.

"Oh, yes, sir; quite sure."

"It was not dark green? Think carefully, now!"

"I don't have to think!" she retorted sharply, with a toss of her head. "Miss Holladay hasn't any dark green gown—nor light one, either. She never wears green—she doesn't like it—it doesn't suit her."

"That will do," said Mr. Royce, and the girl went back to the witness room without understanding in the least the meaning of the questions. "Now, let us have the office-boy again," he said, and that young worthy was called out.

"You say you didn't see the face of that woman who left your office yesterday afternoon?"

"No, sir."

"But you saw her gown?"

"Oh, yes, sir."

"And what color was it?"

"Dark green, sir."

"That will do," said our junior, and sank back in his chair with a sigh of relief. The solution had been under our hands in the morning, and we had missed it! Well, we had found it now. "Gentlemen," he added, his voice a-ring, his face alight, as he sprang to his feet and faced the jury, "I'm ready for your verdict. I wish only to point out that with this one point, the whole case against my client falls to the ground! It was preposterous from the very first!"

He sat down again, and glanced at the coroner.

"Gentlemen of the jury," began Goldberg, "I have merely to remind you that your verdict, whatever it may be, will not finally affect this case. The police authorities will continue their investigations in order that the guilty person may not escape. I conceive that it is not within our province to probe this case further—that may be left to abler and more experienced hands; nor do I think we should inculpate anyone so long as there is a reasonable doubt of his guilt. We await your verdict."

The jury filed slowly out, and I watched them anxiously. In face of the coroner's instructions, they could bring in but one verdict; yet I knew from experience that a jury is ever an unknown quantity, often producing the most unexpected results.

The district attorney came down from his seat and shook hands with both of us.

"That was a great stroke!" he said, with frank admiration. "Whatever made you suspect?"

Mr. Royce handed him the note for answer. He read it through, and stared back at us in astonishment.

"Why," he began, "who wrote this?"

"That's the note that was delivered to us a while ago," answered Mr. Royce. "You know as much about it as we do. But it seems to me a pretty important piece of evidence. I turn it over to you."

"Important!" cried Singleton. "I should say so! Why, gentlemen," and his eyes were gleaming, "this was written either by an accomplice or by the woman herself!"

My chief nodded.

"Precisely," he said. "I'd get on the track of the writer without delay."

Singleton turned and whispered a few words to a clerk, who hurried from the room. Then he motioned to two smooth-faced, well-built men who sat near by, spoke a word to the coroner, and retired with them into the latter's private office. The reporters crowded about us with congratulations and questions. They scented a mystery. What was the matter with Singleton? What was the new piece of evidence? Was it the note? What was in the note?

Mr. Royce smiled.

"Gentlemen," he said, "I trust that my connection with this affair will end in a very few minutes. For any further information, I must refer you to the district attorney—the case is in his hands."

But those men he had summoned into his office were Karle and Johnston, the cleverest detectives on the force. What did he want with them? Mr. Royce merely shrugged his shoulders. Whereat the reporters deserted him and massed themselves before the door into the coroner's room. It opened in a moment, and the two detectives came hurrying out. They looked neither to the right nor left, but shouldered their way cruelly through the crowd, paying not the slightest attention to the questions showered upon them. Then the district attorney came out, and took in the situation at a glance.

"Gentlemen," he said, raising his voice, "I can answer no questions. I must request you to resume your seats, or I shall ask the coroner to clear the room."

They knew that he meant what he said, so they went back to their chairs chagrined, disgusted, biting their nails, striving vainly to work out a solution to the puzzle. It was the coroner's clerk who created a diversion.

"The jury is ready to report, sir," he announced.

"Very well; bring them out," and the jurymen filed slowly back to their seats. I gazed at each face, and cursed the inexpressiveness of the human countenance.

"Have you arrived at a verdict, gentlemen?" asked the coroner.

"We have, sir," answered one of them, and handed a paper to the clerk.

"Is this your verdict, gentlemen?" asked the coroner. "Do you all concur in it?"

They answered in the affirmative as their names were called.

"The clerk will read the verdict," said Goldberg.

Julius stood up and cleared his throat.

"We, the jury," he read, "impaneled in the case of Hiram W. Holladay, deceased, do find that he came to his death from a stab wound in the neck, inflicted by a pen-knife in the hands of a person or persons unknown."

## CHAPTER V: I Dine with a Fascinating Stranger

The coroner dismissed the jury, and came down and shook hands with us.

"I'm going to reward you for your clever work, Mr. Royce," he said. "Will you take the good news to Miss Holladay?"

My chief could not repress the swift flush of pleasure which reddened his cheeks, but he managed to speak unconcernedly.

"Why, yes; certainly. I'll be glad to, if you wish it," he said.

"I do wish it," Goldberg assured him, with a tact and penetration I though admirable. "You may dismiss the policeman who is with her."

Our junior looked inquiringly at the district attorney.

"Before I go," he said, "may I ask what you intend doing, sir?"

"I intend finding the writer of that note," answered Singleton, smiling.

"But, about Miss Holladay?"

Singleton tapped his lips thoughtfully with his pencil.

"Before I answer," he said at last, "I should like to go with you and ask her one question."

"Very well," assented Mr. Royce instantly, and led the way to the room where Miss Holladay awaited us.

She rose with flushing face as we entered, and stood looking at us without speaking; but, despite her admirable composure, I could guess how she was racked with anxiety.

"Miss Holladay," began my chief, "this is Mr. Singleton, the district attorney, who wishes to ask you a few questions."

"One question only," corrected Singleton, bowing. "Were you at your father's office yesterday afternoon, Miss Holladay?"

"No, sir," she answered, instantly and emphatically. "I have not been near my father's office for more than a week."

I saw him studying her for a moment, then he bowed again.

"That is all," he said. "I don't think the evidence justifies me in holding her, Mr. Royce," and he left the room. I followed him, for I knew that I had no further part in our junior's errand. I went back to our table and busied myself gathering together our belongings. The room had gradually cleared, and at the end of ten minutes only the coroner and his clerk remained. They had another case, it seemed, to open in the morning—another case which, perhaps, involved just as great heartache and anguish as ours had. Five minutes later my chief came hurrying back to me, and a glance at his beaming eyes told me how he had been welcomed.

"Miss Holladay has started home with her maid," he said. "She asked me to thank you for her for the great work you did this afternoon, Lester. I told her it was really you who had done everything. Yes, it was!" he added, answering my gesture of denial. "While I was groping helplessly around in the dark, you found the way to the light. But come; we must get back to the office."

We found a cab at the curb, and in a moment were rolling back over the route we had traversed that morning—ages ago, as it seemed to me! It was only a few minutes after three o'clock, and I reflected that I should yet have time to complete the papers in the Hurd case before leaving for the night.

Mr. Graham was still at his desk, and he at once demanded an account of the hearing. I went back to my work, and so caught only a word here and there—enough, however, to show me that our senior was deeply interested in this extraordinary affair. As for me, I put all thought of it resolutely from me, and devoted myself to the work in hand. It was done at last, and I locked my desk with a sigh of relief. Mr. Graham nodded to me kindly as I passed out, and I left the office with the comfortable feeling that I had done a good day's work for myself, as well as for my employers.

A man who had apparently been loitering in the hall followed me into the elevator.

"This is Mr. Lester, isn't it?" he asked, as the car started to descend.

"Yes," I said, looking at him in surprise. He was well dressed, with alert eyes and strong, pleasing face. I had never seen him before.

"And you're going to dinner, aren't you, Mr. Lester?" he continued.

"Yes—to dinner," I assented, more and more surprised.

"Now, don't think me impertinent," he said, smiling at my look of amazement, "but I want you to dine with me this evening. I can promise you as good a meal as you will get at most places in New York."

"But I'm not dressed," I protested.

"That doesn't matter in the least—neither am I, you see. We will dine in a solitude à deux."

"Where?" I questioned.

"Well, how would the Studio suit?"

The car had reached the ground floor, and we left it together. I was completely in the dark as to my companion's purpose, and yet it could have but one explanation—it must be connected in some way with the Holladay case. Unless—and I glanced at him again. No, certainly, he was not a confidence man—even if he was, I would rather welcome the adventure. My curiosity won the battle.

"Very well," I said. "I'll be glad to accept your invitation, Mr.——"

He nodded approvingly.

"There spoke the man of sense. Well, you shall not go unrewarded. Godfrey is my name—no, you don't know me, but I'll soon explain myself. Here's my cab."

I mounted into it, he after me. It seemed to me that there was an unusual number of loiterers about the door of the building, but we were off in a moment, and I did not give them a second thought. We rattled out into Broadway, and turned northward for the three-mile straightaway run to Union Square. I noticed in a moment that we were going at a rate of speed rather exceptional for a cab, and it steadily increased, as the driver found a clear road before him. My companion threw up the trap in the roof of the cab as we swung around into Thirteenth Street.

"All right, Sam?" he called.

The driver grinned down at us through the hole.

"All right, sir," he answered. "They couldn't stand the pace a little bit. They're distanced."

The trap snapped down again, we turned into Sixth Avenue, and stopped in a moment before the Studio—gray and forbidding without, but a dream within. My companion led the way upstairs to a private room, where a table stood ready set for us. The oysters appeared before we were fairly seated.

"You see," he smiled, "I made bold to believe that you'd come with me, and so had the dinner already ordered."

I looked at him without replying. I was completely in the dark. Could this be the writer of the mysterious note? But what could his object be? Above all, why should he so expose himself? He smiled again, as he caught my glance.

"Of course you're puzzled," he said. "Well, I'll make a clean breast of the matter at once. I wanted to talk with you about this Holladay case, and I decided that a dinner at the Studio would be just the ticket."

I nodded. The soup was a thing to marvel at.

"You were right," I assented. "The idea was a stroke of genius."

"I knew you'd think so. You see, since this morning, I've been making rather a study of you. That coup of yours at the coroner's court this afternoon was admirable—one of the best things I ever saw."

I bowed my acknowledgments.

"You were there, then?" I asked.

"Oh, yes; I couldn't afford to miss it."

"The color-blind theory was a simple one."

"So simple that it never occurred to anyone else. I think we're too apt to overlook the simple explanations, which are, after all, nearly always the true ones. It's only in books that we meet the reverse. You remember it's Gaboriau who advises one always to distrust the probable?"

"Yes. I don't agree with him."

"Nor I. Now take this case, for instance. I think it's safe to state that murder, where it's not the result of sudden passion, is always committed for one of two objects—revenge or gain. But Mr. Holladay's past life has been pretty thoroughly probed by the reporters, and nothing has been found to indicate that he had ever made a deadly enemy, at least among the class of people who resort to murder—so that does away with revenge. On the other hand, no one will gain by his death—many will lose by it—in fact, the whole circle of his associates will lose by it. It might seem, at first glance, that his daughter would gain; but I think she loses most of all. She already had all the money she could possibly need; and she's lost her father, whom, it's quite certain, she loved dearly. So what remains?"

"Only one thing," I said, deeply interested in this exposition. "Sudden passion."

He nodded exultantly.

"That's it. Now, who was the woman? From the first I was certain it could not be his daughter—the very thought was preposterous. It seems almost equally absurd, however, to suppose that Holladay could be mixed up with any other woman. He certainly has not been for the last quarter of a century—but before that—well, it's not so certain. And there's one striking point which seems to indicate his guilt."

"Yes—you mean, of course, her resemblance to his daughter."

"Precisely. Such a resemblance must exist—a resemblance unusual, even striking—or it would not for a moment have deceived Rogers. We must remember, however, that Rogers's office was not brilliantly lighted, and that he merely glanced at her. Still, whatever minor differences there may have been, she had the air, the general appearance, the look of Miss Holladay. Mere facial resemblance may happen in a hundred ways, by chance; but the air, the look, the 'altogether' is very different—it indicates a blood relationship. My theory is that she is an illegitimate child, perhaps four or five years older than Miss Holladay."

I paused to consider. The theory was reasonable, and yet it had its faults.

"Now, let's see where this leads us," he continued. "Let us assume that Holladay has been providing for this illegitimate daughter for years. At last, for some reason, he is induced to withdraw this support; or, perhaps, the girl thinks her allowance insufficient. At any rate, after, let us suppose, ineffectual appeals by letter, she does the desperate thing of calling at his office to protest in person. She finds him inexorable—we know his reputation for obstinacy when he had once made up his mind. She reproaches him—she is already desperate, remember—and he answers with that stinging sarcasm for which he was noted. In an ecstacy of anger, she snatches up the knife and stabs him; then, in an agony of remorse, endeavors to check the blood. She sees at last that it is useless, that she cannot save him, and leaves the office. All this is plausible, isn't it?"

"Very plausible," I assented, looking at him in some astonishment. "You forget one thing, however. Rogers testified that he was intimately acquainted with the affairs of his employer, and that he would inevitably have known of any intrigue such as you suggest."

My companion paused for a moment's thought.

"I don't believe that Rogers would so inevitably have known of it," he said, at last. "But, admit that—then there is another theory. Holladay has not been supporting his illegitimate child, who learns of her parentage, and goes to him to demand her rights. That fits the case, doesn't it?"

"Yes," I admitted. "It, also, is plausible."

"It is more than plausible," he said quietly. "Whatever the details may be, the body of the theory itself is unimpeachable—it's the only one which fits the facts. I believe it capable of proof. Don't you see how the note helps to prove it?"

"The note?"

I started at the word, and my suspicions sprang into life again. I looked at him quickly, but his eyes were on the cloth, and he was rolling up innumerable little pellets of bread.

"That note," he added, "proved two things. One was that the writer was deeply interested in Miss Holladay's welfare; the other was that he or she knew Rogers, the clerk, intimately—more than intimately—almost as well as a physician knows an old patient."

"I admit the first," I said. "You'll have to explain the second."

"The second is self-evident. How did the writer of the note know of Rogers's infirmity?"

"His infirmity?"

"Certainly—his color-blindness. I confess, I'm puzzled. How could anyone else know it when Rogers himself didn't know it? That's what I should like to have explained. Perhaps there's only one man or woman in the world who could know—well, that's the one who wrote the note. Now, who is it?"

"But," I began, quickly, then stopped; should I set him right? Or was this a trap he had prepared for me?

His eyes were not on the cloth now, but on me. There was a light in them I did not quite understand. I felt that I must be sure of my ground before I went forward.

"It should be very easy to trace the writer of the note," I said.

"The police have not found it so."

"No?"

"No. It was given to the door-keeper by a boy—just an ordinary boy of from twelve to fourteen years—the man didn't notice him especially. He said there was no answer and went away. How are the police to find that boy? Suppose they do find him? Probably all he could tell them would be that a man stopped him at the corner and gave him a quarter to take the note to the coroner's office."

"He might give a description of the man," I ventured.

"What would a boy's description be worth? It would be, at the best, vague and indefinite. Besides, they've not even found the boy. Now, to return to the note."

We had come to the coffee and cigars, and I felt it time to protest.

"Before we return to the note, Mr. Godfrey," I said, "I'd like to ask you two direct questions. What interest have you in the matter?"

"The interest of every investigator of crime," he answered, smiling.

"You belong to the detective force, then?"

"I have belonged to it. At present, I'm in other employ."

"And what was your object in bringing me here this evening?"

"One portion of my object has been accomplished. The other was to ask you to write out for me a copy of the note."

"But who was it pursued us up Broadway?"

"Oh, I have rivals!" he chuckled. "I flatter myself that was rather neatly done. Will you give me a copy of the note, Mr. Lester?"

"No," I answered squarely. "You'll have to go to the police for that. I'm out of the case."

He bowed across the table to me with a little laugh. As I looked at him, his imperturbable good humor touched me.

"I'll tell you one thing, though," I added. "The writer of the note knew nothing of Rogers's color-blindness—you're off the scent there."

"I am?" he asked amazedly. "Then how did you know it, Mr. Lester?"

"I suppose you detectives would call it deduction—I deduced it."

He took a contemplative puff or two, as he looked at me.

"Well," he exclaimed, at last, "I must say that beats me! Deduced it! That was mighty clever."

Again I bowed my acknowledgments.

"And that's all you can tell me?" he added.

"I'm afraid that's all."

"Very well; thank you for that much," and he flicked the ashes from his cigar. "Now, I fear that I must leave you. I've a good deal of work to do, and you've opened up a very interesting line of speculation. I assure you that I've passed a very pleasant evening. I hope you've not found it tiresome?"

"Quite the contrary," I said heartily. "I've enjoyed myself immensely."

"Then I'll ask one last favor. My cab is at the door. I've no further use for it, and I beg you'll drive home in it."

I saw that he really wished it.

"Why, yes, certainly," I assented.

"Thank you," he said.

He took me down to the door, called the cab, and shook hands with me warmly.

"Good-by, Mr. Lester," he said. "I'm glad of the chance to have met you. I'm not really such a mysterious individual—it's merely a trick of the trade. I hope we'll meet again some time."

"So do I," I said, and meant it.

I saw him stand for a moment on the curb looking after us as we drove away, then he turned and ran rapidly up the steps of the Elevated.

The driver seemed in no hurry to get me home, and I had plenty of time to think over the events of the evening, but I could make nothing of them. What result he had achieved I could not imagine. And yet he had seemed satisfied. As to his theory, I could not but admit that it was an adroit one; even a masterly one—a better one, certainly, than I should have evolved unaided.

The cab drew up at my lodging and I sprang out, tipped the driver, and ran up the steps to the door. My landlady met me on the threshold.

"Oh, Mr. Lester!" she cried. "Such a time as I've had this night! Every five minutes there's been somebody here looking for you, and there's a crowd of them up in your room now. I tried to put them out, but they wouldn't go!"

## CHAPTER VI: Godfrey's Panegyric

I was quite dazed for the moment.

"A crowd of them in my room!" I repeated. "A crowd of whom, Mrs. Fitch?"

"A crowd of reporters! They've been worrying my life out. They seemed to think I had you hid somewhere. I hope you're not in trouble, Mr. Lester?"

"Not the least in the world, my dear madam," I laughed, and I breathed a long sigh of relief, for I had feared I know not what disaster. "I'll soon finish with the reporters," and I went on up the stair.

Long before I reached my rooms, I heard the clatter of voices and caught the odor of various qualities of tobacco. They were lolling about over the furniture, telling stories, I suppose, and they greeted me with a cheer when I entered. They were such jovial fellows that it was quite impossible to feel angry with them—and besides, I knew that they were gentlemen, that they labored early and late at meager salaries, for the pure love of the work; that they were quick to scent fraud or trickery or unworthiness, and inexorable in exposing them; that they loved to do good anonymously, remaining utterly unknown save to the appreciative few behind the scenes. So I returned their greeting smilingly, and sat me down in a chair which one of them obligingly vacated for me.

"Well?" I began, looking about at them.

"My dear Mr. Lester," said the one who had given me the chair, "permit me to introduce myself as Rankin, of the Planet. These gentlemen," and he included them in a wide gesture, "are my colleagues of the press. We've been anxiously awaiting you here in order that we may propound to you certain questions."

"All right; fire away," I said.

"First, we'd like to have your theory of the crime. Your work this afternoon convinced us that you know how to put two and two together, which is more than can be said for the ordinary mortal. The public will want to know your theory—the great public."

"Oh, but I haven't any theory," I protested. "Besides, I don't think the great public is especially interested in me. You see, gentlemen, I'm quite out of the case. When we cleared Miss Holladay, our connection with it ended."

"But is Miss Holladay cleared?" he persisted. "Is it not quite conceivable that in those two hours she was absent from her carriage, she may have changed her gown, gone to her father's office, and then changed back again? In that case, would she not naturally have chosen a green gown, since she never wore green?"

"Oh, nonsense!" I cried. "That's puerile. Either she would disguise herself effectually or not at all. I suppose if you were going to commit a capital crime, you would merely put on a high hat, because you never wear one! I'll tell you this much: I'm morally certain that Miss Holladay is quite innocent. So, I believe, is the district attorney."

"But how about the note, Mr. Lester? What did it contain?"

"Oh, I can't tell you that, you know. It's none of my business."

"But you ought to treat us all alike," he protested.

"I do treat you all alike."

"But didn't Godfrey get it out of you?"

"Godfrey?" I repeated. "Get it out of me?"

He stared at me in astonishment.

"Do you mean to tell me, Mr. Lester," he questioned, "that you haven't been spending the evening with Jim Godfrey, of the Record?"

Then, in a flash, I understood, and as I looked at the rueful faces of the men gathered about me, I laughed until the tears came.

"So it was you," I gasped, "who chased us up Broadway?"

He nodded.

"Yes; but our horses weren't good enough. Where did he take you?"

"To the Studio—Sixth Avenue."

"Of course!" he cried, slapping his leg. "We might have known. Boys, we'd better go back to Podunk."

"Well, at least, Mr. Lester," spoke up another, "you oughtn't to give Godfrey a scoop."

"But I didn't give him a scoop. I didn't even know who he was."

"Didn't you tell him what was in the note?"

"Not a word of it—I told him only one thing."

"And what was that?"

"That the person who wrote the note didn't know that Rogers was color-blind. You are welcome to that statement, too. You see, I'm treating you all alike."

They stood about me, staring down at me, silent with astonishment.

"But," I added, "I think Godfrey suspects what was in the note."

"Why?"

"Well, his theory fits it pretty closely."

"His theory! What is his theory, Mr. Lester?"

"Oh, come," I laughed. "That's telling. It's a good theory, too."

They looked at each other, and, I fancied, gnashed their teeth.

"He seems a pretty clever fellow," I added, just to pile up the agony. "I fancy you'll say so, too, when you see his theory in to-morrow's paper."

"Clever!" cried Rankin. "Why, he's a very fiend of cleverness when it comes to a case of this kind. We're not in the same class with him. He's a fancy fellow—just the Record kind. You're sure you didn't tell him anything else, Mr. Lester?" he added anxiously. "Godfrey's capable of getting a story out of a fence-post."

"No, I'm quite sure I didn't tell him anything else. I only listened to his theory with great interest."

"And assented to it?"

"I said I thought it plausible."

An electric shock seemed to run around the room.

"That's it!" cried Rankin. "That's what he wanted. Now, it isn't his theory any more. It's yours. Oh, I can see his headlines! Won't you tell us what it was?"

I looked up at him.

"Now, frankly, Mr. Rankin," I asked, "if you were in my place, would you tell?"

He hesitated for a moment, and then held out his hand.

"No," he said, as I took it. "I shouldn't. Shake hands, sir; you're all right. Come on, boys, we might as well be going."

They filed out after him, and I heard them go singing up the street. Then I sank back into my chair and thought again of Godfrey's theory; it seemed to fit the case precisely, point by point— even—and I started at the thought—to Miss Holladay's reticence as to her whereabouts the afternoon before. The whole mystery lay plain before me. In some way, she had discovered the existence of her half-sister, had secured her address; she had gone to visit her and had found her away from home—it was probable, even, that the half-sister had written her, asking her to come—though, in that case, why had she not remained at home to receive her? At any rate, Miss Holladay had awaited her return, had noticed her agitation; had, perhaps, even seen certain marks of blood upon her. The news of her father's death had pointed all too clearly to what that agitation and those blood-spots meant. She had remained silent that she might not besmirch her father's name, and also, perhaps, that she might protect the other woman. I felt that I held in my hand the key to the whole problem.

Point by point—but what a snarl it was! That there would be a vigorous search for the other woman I could not doubt, but she had a long start and should easily escape. Yet, perhaps, she had not started—she must have remained in town, else how could that note have been sent to us? She had remained, then—but why? That she should feel any affection for Frances Holladay seemed absurd, and yet, how else explain the note?

I felt that I was getting tangled up in the snarl again—there seemed no limit to its intricacies; so, in very despair, I put the matter from me as completely as I could and went to bed.

The morning's Record attested the truth of Rankin's prophecy. I had grown famous in a night: for Godfrey had, in a measure, made me responsible for his theory, describing me with a wealth of adjectives which I blush to remember, and which I have, even yet, not quite forgiven him. I smiled as I read the first lines:

A Record representative had the pleasure, yesterday evening, of dining with Mr. Warwick Lester, the brilliant young attorney who achieved such a remarkable victory before Coroner Goldberg yesterday afternoon, in the hearing of the Holladay case, and, of course, took occasion to discuss with him the latest developments of this extraordinary crime. Mr. Lester agreed with the Record in a theory which is the only one that fits the facts of the case, and completely and satisfactorily explains all its ramifications.

The theory was then developed at great length and the article concluded with the statement that the Record was assisting the police in a strenuous endeavor to find the guilty woman.

Now that the police knew in which quarter to spread their net, I had little doubt that she would soon be found, since she had tempted providence by remaining in town.

Mr. Graham and Mr. Royce were looking through the Record article when I reached the office, and I explained to them how the alleged interview had been secured. They laughed together in appreciation of Godfrey's audacious enterprise.

"It seems a pretty strong theory," said our senior. "I'm inclined to believe it myself."

I pointed out how it explained Miss Holladay's reticence—her refusal to assist us in proving an alibi. Mr. Royce nodded.

"Precisely. As Godfrey said, the theory touches every point of the case. According to the old police axiom, that proves it's the right one."

### CHAPTER VII: Miss Holladay Becomes Capricious

The body of Hiram Holladay was placed beside that of his wife in his granite mausoleum at Woodlawn on the Sunday following his death; two days later, his will, which had been drawn up by Mr. Graham and deposited in the office safe, was read and duly admitted to probate. As was expected, he had left all his property, without condition or reserve, to his daughter Frances. There were a few bequests to old servants, Rogers receiving a handsome legacy; about half a million was given to various charities in which he had been interested during his life, and the remainder was placed at the absolute disposal of his daughter.

We found that his fortune had been over-estimated, as is usually the case with men whose wealth depends upon the fluctuations of the Street, but there still remained something over four millions for the girl—a pretty dowry. She told us at once that she wished to leave her affairs in our hands, and in financial matters would be guided entirely by our advice. Most of this business was conducted by our junior, and while, of course, he told me nothing, it was evident that Miss Holladay's kindly feelings toward him had suffered no diminution. The whole office was more or less conversant with the affair, and wished him success and happiness.

So a week or ten days passed. The utmost endeavor of newspapers and police had shed no new light on the tragedy, and for the great public it had passed into the background of the forgotten. But for me, at least, it remained of undiminished interest, and more than once I carefully reviewed its features to convince myself anew that our theory was the right one. Only one point occurred to me which would tend to prove it untrue. If there was an illegitimate daughter, the blow she had dealt her father had also deprived her of whatever income he had allowed her, or of any hope of income from him. So she had acted in her own despite—still, Godfrey's theory of sudden passion might explain this away. And then, again, Miss Holladay could probably be counted upon, her first grief past, to provide suitably for her sister. Granting this, the theory seemed to me quite impregnable.

One other thing puzzled me. How had this woman eluded the police? I knew that the French quarter had been ransacked for traces of her, wholly without success, and yet I felt that the search must have been misconducted, else some trace of her would surely have been discovered. Miss Holladay, of course, rigidly refused herself to all inquirers, and here, again, I found myself on the horns of a dilemma. Doubtless, she was very far from wishing the discovery of the guilty woman, and yet I felt that she must be discovered, if only for Miss Holladay's sake, in order to clear away the last vestige of the cloud that shadowed her.

Then came new developments with a startling rapidity. It was toward quitting time one afternoon that a clerk brought word into the inner office that there was a woman without who wished to see Mr. Royce at once. She had given no name, but our junior, who happened to be at leisure for the moment, directed that she be shown in. I recognized her in an instant, and so did he—it was Miss Holladay's maid. I saw, too, that her eyes were red with weeping, and as she sat down beside our junior's desk she began to cry afresh.

"Why, what's the matter?" he demanded. "Nothing wrong with your mistress?"

"She aint my mistress any more," sobbed the girl. "She discharged me this afternoon."

"Discharged you!" echoed our junior. "Why, I thought she thought so much of you?"

"And so did I, sir, but she discharged me just the same."

"But what for?" persisted the other.

"That's just what I don't know, sir; I begged and prayed her to tell me, but she wouldn't even see me. So I came down here. I thought maybe you could help me."

"Well, let me hear about it just as it happened," said Mr. Royce soothingly. "Perhaps I can help you."

"Oh, if you could, sir!" she cried. "You know, I thought the world and all of Miss Frances. I've been with her nearly eight years, and for her to go and treat me like this—why, it just breaks my heart, sir! I dressed her this afternoon about two o'clock, and she was as nice to me as ever—gave me a little brooch, sir, that she was tired of. Then she went out for a drive, and about an hour ago came back. I went right up to her room to undress her, and when I knocked, sir, a strange woman came to the door and said that Miss Frances had engaged her for her maid and wouldn't need me any more, and here was a month's wages. And while I stood there, sir, too dazed to move, she shut the door in my face. After I'd got over it a bit, I begged that I might see Miss Frances, if only to say good-by; but she wouldn't see me. She sent word that she wasn't feeling well, and wouldn't be disturbed."

Her sobs mastered her again and she stopped. I could see the look of amazement on our junior's face, and did not wonder at it. What sudden dislike could her mistress have conceived against this inoffensive and devoted creature?

"You say this other maid was a stranger?" he asked.

"Yes, sir; she'd never been in the house before, so far as I know. Miss Frances brought her back with her in the carriage."

"And what sort of looking woman is she?"

The girl hesitated.

"She looked like a foreigner, sir," she said at last. "A Frenchwoman, maybe, by the way she rolls her r's."

I pricked up my ears. The same thought occurred at that instant to both Mr. Royce and myself.

"Does she resemble Miss Holladay?" he asked quickly.

"Miss Holladay? Oh, no, sir. She's much older—her hair's quite gray."

Well, certainly, Miss Holladay had the right to choose any maid she pleased, and to discharge any or all of her servants; and yet it seemed strangely unlike her to show such seeming injustice to anyone.

"You say she sent down word that she was ill?" said Mr. Royce, at last. "Was she ill when you dressed her?"

"Why, sir," she answered slowly, "I wouldn't exactly say she was ill, but she seemed troubled about something. I think she'd been crying. She's been crying a good deal, off and on, since her father died, poor thing," she added.

That would explain it, certainly; and yet grief for her father might not be the only cause of

Frances Holladay's tears.

"But she didn't seem vexed with you?"

"Oh, no, sir; she gave me a brooch, as I told you."

"I fear I can't promise you anything," said Mr. Royce slowly, after a moment's thought. "Of course, it's none of my business: for Miss Holladay must arrange her household to suit herself; yet, if you don't get back with your old mistress, I may, perhaps, be able to find you a position somewhere else. Suppose you come back in three or four days, and I'll see what I can do."

"All right, sir; and thank you," she said, and left the office.

I had some work of my own to keep me busy that night, so devoted no thought to Frances Holladay and her affairs, but they were recalled to me with renewed force next morning.

"Did you get Miss Holladay's signature to that conveyance?" Mr. Graham chanced to ask his partner in the course of the morning.

"No, sir," answered Mr. Royce, with just a trace of embarrassment. "I called at the house last night, but she sent down word that she was too ill to see me or to transact any business."

"Nothing serious, I hope?" asked the other quickly.

"No, sir; I think not. Just a trace of nervousness probably."

But when he called again at the house that evening, he received a similar message, supplemented with the news imparted by the butler, a servant of many years' standing in the family, that Miss Holladay had suddenly decided to leave the city and open her country place on Long Island. It was only the end of March, and so a full two months and more ahead of the season; but she was feeling very ill, was not able to leave her room, indeed, and believed the fresh air and quiet of the country would do more than anything else to restore her shattered nerves. So the whole household, with the exception of her maid, a cook, house-girl, and under-butler, were to leave the city next day in order to get the country house ready at once.

"I don't wonder she needs a little toning up," remarked our chief sympathetically. "She has gone through a nerve-trying ordeal, especially for a girl reared as she has been. Two or three months of quiet will do her good. When does she expect to leave?"

"In about a week, I think. The time hasn't been definitely set. It will depend upon how the arrangements go forward. It won't be necessary, will it, to bother her with any details of business? That conveyance, for instance——"

"Can wait till she gets back. No, we won't bother her at all."

But it seemed that she had either improved or changed her mind, for two days later a note, which her maid had written for her, came to Mr. Graham, asking him to call upon her in the course of the next twenty-four hours, as she wished to talk over some matters of business with him. It struck me as singular that she should ask for Mr. Graham, but our senior called a cab, and started off at once without comment. An hour later, the door opened, and he entered the office with a most peculiar expression of countenance.

"Well, that beats me!" he exclaimed, as he dropped into his chair.

Our junior wheeled around toward him without speaking, but his anxiety was plain enough.

"To think that a girl as level-headed as Frances Holladay has always been, should suddenly develop such whimsicalities. Yet, I couldn't but admire her grasp of things. Here have I been thinking she didn't know anything about her business and didn't care, but she seems to have kept her eyes open."

"Well?" asked Mr. Royce, as the other paused.

"Well, she started out by reminding me that her property had been left to her absolutely, to do as she pleased with; a point which I, of course, conceded. She then went on to say that she knew of a number of bequests her father had intended to make before his death, and which he would have made if he had not been cut off so suddenly; that the bequests were of such a nature that he did not wish his name to appear in them, and that she was going to undertake to carry them out anonymously."

"Well?" asked our junior again.

"Well," said Mr. Graham slowly, "she asked me to dispose at once of such of her securities as I thought best, in order that I might place in her hands by to-morrow night one hundred thousand dollars in cash—a cool hundred thousand!"

## CHAPTER VIII: The Mysterious Maid

"A hundred thousand dollars!" ejaculated Mr. Royce, and sat staring at his chief.

"A hundred thousand dollars! That's a good deal for a girl to give away in a lump, but she can afford it. Of course, we've nothing to do but carry out her instructions. I think both of us can guess what she intends doing with the money."

The other nodded. I believed that I could guess, too. The money, of course, was intended for the other woman—she was not to suffer for her crime, after all. Miss Holladay seemed to me in no little danger of becoming an accessory after the fact.

"She seems really ill," continued our senior. "She looks thinner and quite careworn. I commended her resolution to seek rest and quiet and change of scene."

"When does she go, sir?" asked Mr. Royce, in a subdued voice.

"The day after to-morrow, I think. She did not say definitely. In fact, she could talk very little. She's managed to catch cold—the grip, I suppose—and was very hoarse. It would have been cruelty to make her talk, and I didn't try."

He wheeled around to his desk, and then suddenly back again.

"By the way," he said, "I saw the new maid. I can't say I wholly approve of her."

He paused a minute, weighing his words.

"She seems careful and devoted," he went on, at last, "but I don't like her eyes. They're too intense. I caught her two or three times watching me strangely. I can't imagine where Miss Holladay picked her up, or why she should have picked her up at all. She's French, of course—she speaks with a decided accent. About the money, I suppose we'd better sell a block of U. P. bonds. They're the least productive of her securities."

"Yes, I suppose so," agreed Mr. Royce, and the chief called up a broker and gave the necessary orders. Then he turned to other work, and the day passed without any further reference to Miss Holladay or her affairs.

The proceeds of the sale were brought to the office early the next afternoon, a small packet neatly sealed and docketed—one hundred thousand-dollar bills. Mr. Graham turned it over in his hand thoughtfully.

"You'll take it to the house, of course, John," he said to his partner. "Lester 'd better go with you."

So Mr. Royce placed the package in his pocket, a cab was summoned, and we were off. The trip was made without incident, and at the end of half an hour we drew up before the Holladay mansion.

It was one of the old-styled brownstone fronts which lined both sides of the avenue twenty years ago; it was no longer in the ultra-fashionable quarter, which had moved up toward Central Park, and shops of various kinds were beginning to encroach upon the neighborhood; but it had been Hiram Holladay's home for forty years, and he had never been willing to part with it. At this moment all the blinds were down and the house had a deserted look. We mounted the steps to the door, which was opened at once to our ring by a woman whom I knew instinctively to be the new maid, though she looked much less like a maid than like an elderly working-woman of the middle class.

"We've brought the money Miss Holladay asked Mr. Graham for yesterday," said Mr. Royce. "I'm John Royce, his partner," and without answering the woman motioned us in. "Of course we must have a receipt for it," he added. "I have it ready here, and she need only attach her signature."

"Miss Holladay is too ill to see you, sir," said the maid, with careful enunciation. "I will myself the paper take to her and get her signature."

Mr. Royce hesitated a moment in perplexity. As for me, I was ransacking my memory—where had I heard that voice before? Somewhere, I was certain—a voice low, vibrant, repressed, full of color. Then, with a start, I remembered! It was Miss Holladay's voice, as she had risen to welcome our junior that morning at the coroner's court! I shook myself together—for that was nonsense!

"I fear that won't do," said Mr. Royce at last. "The sum is a considerable one, and must be given to Miss Holladay by me personally in the presence of this witness."

It was the maid's turn to hesitate; I saw her lips tighten ominously.

"Very well, sir," she said. "But I warn you, she is most nervous and it has been forbidden her to talk."

"She will not be called upon to talk," retorted Mr. Royce curtly; and without answering, the woman turned and led the way up the stair and to her mistress's room.

Miss Holladay was lying back in a great chair with a bandage about her head, and even in the half-light I could see how changed she was. She seemed much thinner and older, and coughed occasionally in a way that frightened me. Not grief alone, I told myself, could have caused this breakdown; it was the secret weighing upon her. My companion noted the change, too, of course—a greater change, perhaps, than my eyes could perceive—and I saw how moved and shocked he was.

"My dear Miss Holladay," he began, but she stopped him abruptly with a little imperative motion of the hand.

"Pray do not," she whispered hoarsely. "Pray do not."

He stopped and pulled himself together. When he spoke again, it was in quite a different tone. "I have brought the money you asked for," and he handed her the package.

"Thank you," she murmured.

"Will you verify the amount?"

"Oh, no; that is not necessary."

"I have a receipt here," and he produced it and his fountain-pen. "Please sign it."

She took the pen with trembling fingers, laid the receipt upon her chair-arm without reading, and signed her name with a somewhat painful slowness. Then she leaned back with a sigh of relief, and buried her face in her hands. Mr. Royce placed the receipt in his pocket book, and stopped, hesitating. But the maid had opened the door and was awaiting us. Her mistress made no sign; there was no excuse to linger. We turned and followed the maid.

"Miss Holladay seems very ill," said Mr. Royce, in a voice somewhat tremulous, as she paused before us in the lower hall.

"Yes, sir; ver' ill."

Again the voice! I took advantage of the chance to look at her intently. Her hair was turning gray, certainly; her face was seamed with lines which only care and poverty could have graven there; and yet, beneath it all, I fancied I could detect a faded but living likeness to Hiram Holladay's daughter. I looked again—it was faint, uncertain—perhaps my nerves were overwrought and were deceiving me. For how could such a likeness possibly exist?

"She has a physician, of course?" asked my companion.

"Oh, yes, sir."

"He has advised rest and quiet?"

"Yes, sir."

"When do you leave for the country?"

"To-morrow or the next day after that, I think, sir."

He turned to the door and then paused, hesitating. He opened his lips to say something more— his anxiety was clamoring for utterance—then he changed his mind and stepped outside as she held the door open.

"Good-day," he said, with stern repression. "I wish her a pleasant journey."

The door closed after us, and we went down the steps.

"Jenkinson's the family doctor," he said. "Let's drive around there, and find out how really ill Miss Holladay is. I'm worried about her, Lester."

"That's a good idea," I agreed, and gave the driver the address. Jenkinson was in his office, and received us at once.

"Doctor Jenkinson," began our junior, without preamble, "I am John Royce, of Graham & Royce. You know, I suppose, that we are the legal advisers of Miss Frances Holladay."

"Yes," answered Jenkinson. "Glad to meet you, Mr. Royce."

"In consequence, we're naturally interested in her welfare and all that concerns her, and I called to ask you for some definite details of her condition."

"Her condition? I don't quite understand."

"We should like to know, doctor, just how ill she is."

"Ill!" repeated Jenkinson, in evident surprise. "But is she ill?"

"She's your patient, isn't she? I thought you were the family doctor."

"So I am," assented the other. "But I haven't seen Miss Holladay for ten days or two weeks. At that time, she seemed quite well—a little nervous, perhaps, and worried, but certainly not requiring medical attention. She has always been unusually robust."

Mr. Royce stopped, perplexed; as for me, my head was in a whirl again.

"I'll tell you the story," he said at last. "I should like the benefit of your advice;" and he recounted rapidly the facts of Miss Holladay's illness, in so far as he knew them, ending with an account of our recent visit, and the statement of the maid that her mistress was under a doctor's care. Jenkinson heard him to the end without interrupting, but he was plainly puzzled and annoyed.

"And you say she looked very ill?" he asked.

"Oh, very ill, sir; alarmingly ill, to my unpracticed eyes. She seemed thin and worn—she could scarcely talk—she had such a cough—I hardly knew her."

Again the doctor paused to consider. He was a very famous doctor, with many very famous patients, and I could see that this case piqued him—that another physician should have been preferred!

"Of course, Mr. Royce," he said finally, "Miss Holladay was perfectly free to choose another physician, if she thought best."

"But would you have thought it probable?" queried our junior.

"Ten minutes ago, I should have thought it extremely improbable," answered the doctor emphatically. "Still, women are sometimes erratic, as we doctors know to our sorrow."

Mr. Royce hesitated, and then took the bull by the horns.

"Doctor Jenkinson," he began earnestly, "don't you think it would be wise to see Miss Holladay—you know how her father trusted you, and relied on you—and assure yourself that she's in good hands? I confess, I don't know what to think, but I fear some danger is hanging over her. Perhaps she may even have fallen into the hands of the faith-curists."

Jenkinson smiled.

"The advice to seek rest and quiet seems sane enough," he said, "and utterly unlike any that a faith-curist would give."

"But still, if you could see for yourself," persisted Mr. Royce.

The doctor hesitated, drumming with his fingers upon the arm of his chair.

"Such a course would be somewhat unprofessional," he said at last. "Still, I might call in a merely social way. My interest in the family would, I think, excuse me."

Mr. Royce's face brightened, and he caught the doctor's hand.

"Thank you, sir," he said warmly. "It will lift a great anxiety from the firm, and, I may add, from me, personally."

The doctor laughed good-naturedly.

"I knew that, of course," he said. "We doctors hear all the gossip going. I might add that I was glad to hear this bit. If you'll wait for me here, I'll go at once."

We instantly assented, and he called his carriage, and was driven away. I felt that, at last, we were to see behind one corner of the curtain—perhaps one glimpse would be enough to penetrate the mystery. But, in half an hour he was back again, and a glance at his face told me that we were again destined to disappointment.

"I sent up my card," he reported briefly, "and Miss Holladay sent down word that she must beg to be excused."

Mr. Royce's face fell.

"And that was all?" he asked.

"That was all. Of course, there was nothing for me to do but come away. I couldn't insist on seeing her."

"No," assented the other. "No. How do you explain it, doctor?"

Jenkinson sat down, and for a moment studied the pattern of the carpet.

"Frankly, Mr. Royce," he said at last, "I don't know how to explain it. The most probable explanation is that Miss Holladay is suffering from some form of dementia—perhaps only acute primary dementia, which is usually merely temporary—but which may easily grow serious, and even become permanent."

The theory had occurred to me, and I saw from the expression of Mr. Royce's face that he, also, had thought of it.

"Is there no way that we can make sure?" he asked. "She may need to be saved from herself."

"She may need it very badly," agreed the doctor, nodding. "Yet, she is of legal age, and absolute mistress of her actions. There are no relatives to interfere—no intimate friends, even, that I know of. I see no way unless you, as her legal adviser, apply to the authorities for an inquest of lunacy."

But Mr. Royce made an instant gesture of repugnance.

"Oh, that's absurd!" he cried. "We have no possible reason to take such action. It would offend her mortally."

"No doubt," assented the other. "So I fear that at present nothing can be done—things will just have to take their course till something more decided happens."

"There's no tendency to mental disease in the family?" inquired Mr. Royce, after a moment.

"Not the slightest," said the doctor emphatically. "Her father and mother were both sound and well-balanced. I know the history of the family through three generations, and there's no hint of any taint. Twenty-five years ago Holladay, who was then just working to the top in Wall Street, drove himself too hard—it was when the market went all to pieces over that Central Pacific deal—and had a touch of apoplexy. It was just a touch, but I made him take a long vacation, which he spent abroad with his wife. It was then, by the way, that his daughter was born. Since then he has been careful, and has never been bothered with a recurrence of the trouble. In fact, that's the only illness in the least serious I ever knew him to have."

There was nothing more to be said, and we turned to go.

"If there are any further developments," added the doctor, as he opened the door, "will you let me know? You may count upon me, if I can be of any assistance."

"Certainly," answered our junior. "You're very kind, sir," and we went back to our cab.

The week that followed was a perplexing one for me, and a miserable one for Royce. As I know now, he had written her half a dozen times, and had received not a single word of answer. For myself, I had discovered one more development of the mystery. On the day following the delivery of the money, I had glanced, as usual, through the financial column of the Sun as I rode home on the car, and one item had attracted my attention. The brokerage firm of Swift & Currer had that day presented at the sub-treasury the sum of one hundred thousand dollars in currency for conversion into gold. An inquiry at their office next morning elicited the fact that the exchange had been effected for the account of Miss Frances Holladay. It was done, of course, that the recipient of the money might remain beyond trace of the police.

## CHAPTER IX: I Meet Monsieur Martigny

Our regular work at the office just at that time happened to be unusually heavy and trying. The Brown injunction suit, while not greatly attracting public attention, involved points of such nicety and affected interests so widespread, that the whole bar of New York was watching it. The Hurd substitution case was more spectacular, and appealed to the press with peculiar force, since one of the principal victims had been the eldest son of Preston McLandberg, the veteran managing editor of the Record, and the bringing of the suit impugned the honor of his family— but it is still too fresh in the public mind to need recapitulation here, even were it connected with this story. The incessant strain told upon both our partners and even upon me, so that I returned to my rooms after dinner one evening determined to go early to bed. But I had scarcely donned my house-coat, settled in my chair, and got my pipe to going, when there came a tap at the door.

"Come in," I called, thinking it was Mrs. Fitch, my landlady, and too weary to get up.

But it was not Mrs. Fitch's pale countenance, with its crown of gray hair, which appeared in the doorway; it was a rotund and exceedingly florid visage.

"You will pardon me, sir," began a resonant voice, which I instantly remembered, even before the short, square figure stepped over the threshold into the full light, "but I have just discovered that I have no match with which to ignite my gas. If I might from you borrow one——"

"Help yourself," I said, and held out to him my case, which was lying on the table at my elbow.

"You are very good," he said, and then, as he stepped forward and saw me more distinctly, he uttered a little exclamation of surprise. "Ah, it is Mistair——"

"Lester," I added, seeing that he hesitated.

"It is a great pleasure," he was saying, as he took the matches; "a great good fortune which brought me to this house. So lonely one grows at times—and then, I greatly desire some advice. If you would have the leisure——"

"Certainly," and I waved toward a chair. "Sit down."

"In one moment," he said. "You will pardon me," and he disappeared through the doorway.

He was back almost at once with a handful of cigarettes, which he placed on the table. Then he drew up a chair. With a little deprecatory gesture, he used one of my matches to light a cigarette.

"It was truly for the gas," he said, catching my smile; "and the gas for the cigarette!"

There was something fascinating about the man; an air of good-humor, of comradeship, of strength, of purpose. My eyes were caught by his stodgy, nervous hands, as he held the match to his cigarette; then they wandered to his face—to the black hair flecked here and there with gray; to the bright, deep-set eyes, ambushed under heavy brows; to the full lips, which the carefully arranged mustache did not at all conceal; to the projecting chin, with its little plume of an imperial. A strong face and a not unhandsome one, with a certain look of mastery about it——

"It is true that I need advice," he was saying, as he slowly exhaled a great puff of smoke which he had drawn deep into his lungs. "My name is Martigny—Jasper Martigny"—I nodded by way of salutation—"and I am from France, as you have doubtless long since suspected. It is my desire to become a citizen of Amer-ric'."

"How long have you been living in America?" I asked.

"Since two months only. It is my intention to establish here a business in wines."

"Well," I explained, "you can take no steps toward naturalization for three years. Then you go before a court and make a declaration of your intentions. Two years later, you will get your papers."

"You mean," he hesitated, "that it takes so many years——"

"Five years' actual residence—yes."

"But," and he hesitated again, "I had understood that—that——"

"That it was easier? There are illegal ways, of course; but you can scarcely expect me to advise you concerning them, Mr. Martigny."

"No; of course, no!" he cried hastily, waving his hand in disclaimer. "I did not know—it makes nothing to me—I will wait—I wish to obey the laws."

He picked up a fresh cigarette, lit it from the other, and tossed away the end.

"Will you not try one?" he asked, seeing that my pipe was finished, and I presently found myself enjoying the best cigarette I had ever smoked. "You comprehend French—no?"

"Not well enough to enjoy it," I said.

"I am sorry—I believe you would like this book which I am reading," and he pulled a somewhat tattered volume from his pocket. "I have read it, oh, ver' many times, as well as all the others—though this, of course, is the masterpiece."

He held it so that I could see the title. It was "Monsieur Lecoq."

"I have read it in English," I said.

"And did you not like it—yes? I am ver' fond of stories of detection. That is why I was so absorbed in that affair of Mees—Mees—ah, I have forgotten! Your names are so difficult for me."

"Miss Holladay," I said.

"Ah, yes; and has that mystery ever arrived at a solution?"

"No," I said. "Unfortunately, we haven't any Monsieur Lecoqs on our detective force."

"Ah, no," he smiled. "And the young lady—in her I conceived a great interest, even though I did not see her—how is she?"

"The shock was a little too much for her," I said. "She's gone out to her country-place to rest. She'll soon be all right again, I hope."

He had taken a third cigarette, and was lighting it carelessly, with his face half-turned away from me. I noticed how flushed his neck was.

"Oh, undoubtedly," he agreed, after a moment; "at least, I should be most sad to think otherwise. But it is late; I perceive that you are weary; I thank you for your kindness."

"Not at all," I protested. "I hope you'll come in whenever you feel lonely."

"A thousand thanks! I shall avail myself of your invitation. My apartment is just across the hall," he added, as I opened the door. "I trust to see you there."

"You shall," I said heartily, and bade him good-night.

In the week that followed, I saw a good deal of Martigny. I would meet him on the stairs or in the hall; he came again to see me, and I returned his visit two nights later, upon which occasion he produced two bottles of Château Yquem of a delicacy beyond all praise. And I grew more and more to like him—he told me many stories of Paris, which, it seemed, had always been his home, with a wit to which his slight accent and formal utterance gave new point; he displayed a kindly interest in my plans which was very pleasing; he was always tactful, courteous, good-humored. He was plainly a boulevardier, a man of the world, with an outlook upon life a little startling in its materiality, but interesting in its freshness, and often amusing in its frankness. And he seemed to return my liking—certainly it was he who sought me, not I who sought him. He was being delayed, he explained, in establishing his business; he could not get just the quarters he desired, but in another week there would be a place vacant. He would ask me to draw up the lease. Meanwhile, time hung rather heavily on his hands.

"Though I do not quarrel with that," he added, sitting in my room one evening. "It is necessary for me that I take life easily. I have a weakness of the heart, which has already given me much trouble. Besides, I have your companionship, which is most welcome, and for which I thank you. I trust Mees—Mees—what you call—Holladay is again well."

"We haven't heard from her," I said. "She is still at her place in the country."

"Oh, she is doubtless well—in her I take such an interest—you will pardon me if I weary you."

"Weary me? But you don't!"

"Then I will make bold to ask you—have you made any—what you call—theory of the crime?"

"No," I answered; "that is, none beyond what was in the newspapers—the illegitimate daughter theory. I suppose you saw it. That seems to fit the case."

He nodded meditatively. "Yet I like to imagine how Monsieur Lecoq would approach it. Would he believe it was a murder simply because it so appeared? Has it occurred to you that Mees Holladay truly might have visited her father, and that his death was not a murder at all, but an accident?"

"An accident?" I repeated. "How could it be an accident? How could a man be stabbed accidentally in the neck? Besides, even if it were an accident, how would that explain his daughter's rushing from the building without trying to save him, without giving the alarm? If it wasn't a murder, why should the woman, whoever she was, be frightened? How else can you explain her flight?"

He was looking at me thoughtfully. "All that you say is ver' true," he said. "It shows that you have given to the case much thought. I believe that you also have a fondness for crimes of mystery," and he smiled at me. "Is it not so, Mistair Lester?"

"I had never suspected it," I laughed, "until this case came up, but the microbe seems to have bitten me."

"Ah, yes," he said doubtfully, not quite understanding.

"And I've rather fancied at times," I admitted, "that I should like to take a hand at solving it—though, of course, I never shall. Our connection with the case is ended."

He shot me a quick glance, then lighted another cigarette.

"Suppose it were assigned to you to solve it," he asked, "how would you set about it?"

"I'd try to find the mysterious woman."

"But the police, so I understand, attempted that and failed," he objected. "How could you succeed?"

"Oh, I dare say I shouldn't succeed," I laughed, his air striking me as a little more earnest than the occasion demanded. "I should probably fail, just as the police did."

"In France," he remarked, "it is not in the least expected that men of the law should——"

"Nor is it here," I explained. "Only, of course, a lawyer can't help it, sometimes; some cases demand more or less detective work, and are yet too delicate to be intrusted to the police."

"It is also the fault of our police that it is too fond of the newspapers, of posing before the public—it is a fault of human nature, is it not?"

"You speak English so well, Mr. Martigny," I said, "that I have wondered where you learned it."

"I was some years in England—the business of wine—and devoted myself seriously to the study of the language. But I still find it sometimes very difficult to understand you Americans— you speak so much more rapidly than the English, and so much less distinctly. You have a way of running your words together, of dropping whole syllables——"

"Yes," I smiled, "and that is the very thing we complain of in the French."

"Oh, our elisions are governed by well-defined laws which each one comprehends, while here——"

"Every man is a law unto himself. Remember, it is the land of the free——"

"And the home of the license, is it not?" he added, unconscious of irony.

Yes, I decided, I was very fortunate in gaining Martigny's acquaintance. Of course, after he opened his business, he would have less time to devote to me; but, nevertheless, we should have many pleasant evenings together, and I looked forward to them with considerable anticipation. He was interesting in himself—entertaining, with that large tolerance and good humor which I have already mentioned, and which was one of the most striking characteristics of the man. And then—shall I admit it?—I was lonely, too, sometimes, as I suppose every bachelor must be; and I welcomed a companion.

It was Monday, the fourteenth day of April, and we had just opened the office, when a clerk hurried in with a message for Mr. Royce.

"There's a man out here who wants to see you at once, sir," he said. "He says his name's Thompson, and that he's Miss Frances Holladay's butler."

Our junior half-started from his chair in his excitement; then he controlled himself, and sank back into it again.

"Show him in," he said, and sat with his eyes on the door, haggard in appearance, pitiful in his eagerness. Not until that moment had I noticed how the past week had aged him and worn him down—his work, of course, might account for part of it, but not for all. He seemed almost ill.

The door opened in a moment, and a gray-haired man of about sixty entered. He was fairly gasping for breath, and plainly laboring under strong emotion.

"Well, Thompson," demanded Mr. Royce, "what's the trouble now?"

"Trouble enough, sir!" cried the other. "My mistress has been made away with, sir! She left town just ten days ago for Belair, where we were all waiting for her, and nobody has set eyes on her since, sir!"

## CHAPTER X: An Astonishing Disappearance

Mr. Royce grasped the arms of his chair convulsively, and remained for a moment speechless under the shock. Then he swung around toward me.

"Come here, Lester," he said hoarsely. "I needed you once before, and I need you now. This touches me so closely I can't think consecutively. You will help, won't you?"

There was an appeal in his face which showed his sudden weakness—an appeal there was no resisting, even had I not, myself, been deeply interested in the case.

"Gladly," I answered, from the depths of my heart, seeing how overwrought he was. "I'll help to the very limit of my power, Mr. Royce."

He sank back into his chair again, and breathed a long sigh.

"I knew you would," he said. "Get the story from Thompson, will you?"

I brought a chair, and sat down by the old butler.

"You have been in Mr. Holladay's family a great many years, haven't you, Mr. Thompson?" I asked, to give him opportunity to compose himself.

"Yes, a great many years, sir—nearly forty, I should say."

"Before Miss Holladay's birth, then?"

"Oh, yes, sir; long before. Just before his marriage, Mr. Holladay bought the Fifth Avenue house he lived in ever since, and I was employed, then, sir, as an under-servant."

"Mr. Holladay and his wife were very happy together, weren't they?" I questioned.

"Very happy; yes, sir. They were just like lovers, sir, until her death. They seemed just made for each other, sir," and the trite old saying gathered a new dignity as he uttered it.

I paused a moment to consider. This, certainly, seemed to discredit the theory that Holladay had ever had a liaison with any other woman, and yet what other theory was tenable?

"There was nothing to mar their happiness that you know of? Of course," I added, "you understand, Thompson, that I'm not asking these questions from idle curiosity, but to get to the bottom of this mystery, if possible."

"I understand, sir," he nodded. "No, there was nothing to mar their happiness—except one thing."

"And what was that?"

"Why, they had no children, sir, for fifteen years and more. After Miss Frances came, of course, that was all changed."

"She was born abroad?"

"Yes, sir; in France. I don't just know the town."

"But you know the date of her birth?"

"Oh, yes, sir—the tenth of June, eighteen seventy-six—we always celebrated it."

"Mr. Holladay was with his wife at the time?"

"Yes, sir; he and his wife had been abroad nearly a year. His health had broken down, and the doctor made him take a long vacation. He came home a few months later, but Mrs. Holladay stayed on. She didn't get strong again, some way. She stayed nearly four years, and he went over every few months to spend a week with her; and at last she came home to die, bringing her child with her. That was the first time any of us ever saw Miss Frances."

"Mr. Holladay thought a great deal of her?"

"You may well say so, sir; she took his wife's place," said the old man simply.

"And she thought a great deal of him?"

"More than that, sir; she fairly worshiped him. She was always at the door to meet him; always dined with him; they almost always spent their evenings together. She didn't care much for society—I've often heard her tell him that she'd much rather just stay at home with him. It was he who rather insisted on her going out; for he was proud of her, as he'd a right to be."

"Yes," I said: for all this fitted in exactly with what I had always heard about the family. "There were no other relatives, were there?"

"None at all, sir; both Mr. Holladay and his wife were only children; their parents, of course, have been dead for years."

"Nor any intimate friends?"

"None I'd call intimate, sir; Miss Frances had some school friends, but she was always—well—reserved, sir."

"Yes." I nodded again. "And now," I added, "tell me, as fully as you can, what has happened within the last three weeks."

"Well, sir," he began slowly, "after her father's death, she seemed quite distracted for a while—wandered about the house, sat in the library of evenings, ate scarcely anything. Then Mr. Royce got to coming to the house, and she brightened up, and we all hoped she'd soon be all right again. Then she seemed to get worse of a sudden, and sent us all away to get Belair ready. I got the place in order, sir, and telegraphed her that we were ready. She answered that she'd come in a few days. Ten days ago the rest of the servants came, and I looked for her every day, but she didn't come. I telegraphed her again, but she didn't answer, and, finally, I got so uneasy, sir, I couldn't rest, and came back to the city to see what was the matter. I got here early this morning, and went right to the house. Thomas, the second butler, had been left in charge, and he told me that Miss Frances and her maid had started for Belair the same day the servants did. That's all I know."

"Then she's been gone ten days?" I questioned.

"Ten days; yes, sir."

Ten days! What might not have happened in that time! Doctor. Jenkinson's theory of dementia recurred to me, and I was more than ever inclined to credit it. How else explain this flight? I could see from Mr. Royce's face how absolutely nonplused he was.

"Well," I said at last, for want of something better, "we'll go with you to the house, and see the man in charge there. Perhaps he can tell us something more."

But he could tell us very little. Ten days before, a carriage had driven up to the door, Miss Holladay and her maid had entered it and been driven away. The carriage had been called, he thought, from some neighboring stable, as the family coachman had been sent away with the other servants. They had driven down the avenue toward Thirty-fourth Street, where, he supposed, they were going to the Long Island station. We looked through the house—it was in perfect order. Miss Holladay's rooms were just as she would naturally have left them. Her father's rooms, too, were evidently undisturbed.

"Here's one thing," I said, "that might help," and I picked up a photograph from the mantel. "You won't mind my using it?"

Mr. Royce took it with trembling hand and gazed at it for a moment—at the dark eyes, the earnest mouth——Then he handed it back to me.

"No," he answered; "not if it will really help; we must use every means we can. Only——"

"I won't use it unless I absolutely have to," I assured him; "and when I'm done with it, I'll destroy it."

"Very well," he assented, and I put it in my pocket.

There was nothing more to be discovered there, and we went away, after warning the two men to say not a word to anyone concerning their mistress's disappearance.

Plainly, the first thing to be done was to find the coachman who had driven Miss Holladay and her maid away from the house; and with this end in view, we visited all the stables in the neighborhood; but from none of them had a carriage been ordered by her. Had she ordered it herself from a stable in some distant portion of the city for the purpose of concealing her whereabouts, or had it been ordered for her by her maid, and was she really the victim of foul play? I put this question to Mr. Royce, but he seemed quite unable to reach a conclusion. As for myself, I was certain that she had gone away of her own accord, and had deliberately planned her disappearance. Why? Well, I began to suspect that we had not yet really touched the bottom of the mystery.

We drove back to the office, and found Mr. Graham there. I related to him the circumstances of our search, and submitted to him and to our junior one question for immediate settlement.

"At the best, it's a delicate case," I pointed out. "Miss Holladay has plainly laid her plans very carefully to prevent us following her. It may be difficult to prove that she has not gone away entirely of her own accord. She certainly has a perfect right to go wherever she wishes without consulting us. Have we the right to follow her against her evident desire?"

For a moment Mr. Graham did not answer, but sat tapping his desk with that deep line of perplexity between his eyebrows. Then he nodded emphatically.

"It's our duty to follow her and find her," he said. "It's perfectly evident to me that no girl in her right mind would act as she has done. She had no reason whatever for deceiving us—for running away. We wouldn't have interfered with her. Jenkinson's right—she's suffering with dementia. We must see that she receives proper medical treatment."

"It might not be dementia," I suggested, "so much as undue influence—on the part of the new maid, perhaps."

"Then it's our duty to rescue her from that influence," rejoined Mr. Graham, "and restore her to her normal mentality."

"Even if we offend her?"

"We can't stop to think of that. Besides, she won't be offended when she comes to herself. The question is, how to find her most speedily."

"The police, probably, could do it most speedily," I said; "but since she can be in no immediate danger of any kind, I rather doubt whether it would be wise to call in the police. Miss Holladay would very properly resent any more publicity——"

"But," objected Mr. Graham, "if we don't call in the police, how are we to find her? I recognize, of course, how undesirable it is that she should be subjected to any further notoriety, but is there any other way?"

I glanced at Mr. Royce, and saw that he was seemingly sunk in apathy.

"If I could be excused from the office for a few days, sir," I began hesitatingly, "I might be able to find some trace of her. If I'm unsuccessful, we might then call in the authorities."

Mr. Royce brightened up for a moment.

"That's it," he said. "Let Lester look into it."

"Very well," assented Mr. Graham. "I agree to that. Of course, any expenses you may incur will be borne by the office."

"Thank you, sir," and I rose with fast-beating heart, for the adventure appealed to me strongly. "I'll begin at once then. I should like assistance in one thing. Could you let me have three or four clerks to visit the various stables of the city? It would be best, I think, to use our own people."

"Certainly," assented our senior instantly. "I'll call them in, and we can give them their instructions at once."

So four clerks were summoned, and each was given a district of the city. Their instructions were to find from which stable Miss Holladay had ordered a carriage on the morning of Thursday, April 3d. They were to report at the office every day, noon and evening, until the search was finished. They started away at once, and I turned to follow them, when my eye was caught by the expression of our junior's face.

"Mr. Royce is ill, sir!" I cried. "Look at him!"

He was leaning forward heavily, his face drawn and livid, his eyes set, his hands plucking at the arms of his chair. We sprang to him and led him to a couch. I bathed his hands and face in cold water, while Mr. Graham hurriedly summoned a physician. The doctor soon arrived, and diagnosed the case at a glance.

"Nervous breakdown," he said tersely. "You lawyers drive yourselves too hard. It's a wonder to me you don't all drop over. We'll have to look out, or this will end in brain fever."

He poured out a stimulant, which the sick man swallowed without protest. He seemed stronger in a few moments, and began talking incoherently to himself. We got him down to the doctor's carriage, and drove rapidly to his lodgings, where we put him to bed without delay.

"I think he'll pull through," observed the doctor, after watching him for a while. "I'll get a couple of nurses, and we'll give him every chance. Has he any relatives here in New York?"

"No; his relatives are all in Ohio. Had they better be notified?"

"Oh, I think not—not unless he gets worse. He seems to be naturally strong. I suppose he's been worrying about something?"

"Yes," I said. "He has been greatly worried by one of his cases."

"Of course," he nodded. "If the human race had sense enough to stop worrying, there'd be mighty little work for us doctors."

"I'd like to call Doctor Jenkinson into the case," I said. "He knows Mr. Royce, and may be of help."

"Certainly; I'll be glad to consult with Doctor Jenkinson."

So Jenkinson was called, and confirmed the diagnosis. He understood, of course, the cause of Mr. Royce's breakdown, and turned to me when the consultation was ended, and his colleague had taken his departure.

"Mr. Lester," he said, "I advise you to go home and get some rest. Put this case out of your mind, or you'll be right where Mr. Royce is. He had some more bad news, I suppose?"

I told him of Miss Holladay's disappearance; he pondered over it a moment with grave face.

"This strengthens my belief that she is suffering with dementia," he said. "Sudden aversion to relatives and friends is one of its most common symptoms. Of course, she must be found."

"I'm going to find her," I assured him, with perhaps a little more confidence than I really felt.

"Well, remember to call on me if I can help you. But first of all, go home and sleep for ten hours—twelve, if you can. Mind, no work before that—no building of theories. You'll be so much the fresher to-morrow."

I recognized the wisdom of this advice, but I had one thing to do first. I took a cab and drove to the nearest telegraph office. There I sent an imperative message to Brooks, the Holladay coachman, telling him to return to New York by the first train, and report to me at the office. That done, I gave the driver my address and settled back in the seat.

No building of theories, Jenkinson had said; yet it was difficult to keep the brain idle. Where was Frances Holladay? Why had she fled? Was she really mentally deranged? Had the weight of the secret proved too great for her? Or had she merely fallen under the influence of the woman who was guilty? Supposing she was insane, what should we do with her when we found her? How could we control her? And, supposing she were not insane, what legal right had we to interfere with her? These and a hundred other questions crowded upon me, till thought failed, and I lay back confused, indifferent——

"Here we are, sir," said the driver, jumping down from his seat and jerking open the door.

I paid him, and went stumblingly up the steps. I have no doubt he was grinning behind me. As I fumbled with my key, someone opened the door from the inside.

"Why, Mistair Lester!" exclaimed Martigny's voice. "What is it? You have no illness, I hope!"

"No," I murmured, "I'm just dead tired," and I started blindly for the stair.

"Let me assist you," and he took my arm and helped me up; then went on ahead, opened my door, and lighted the gas.

"Thanks," I said, as I dropped into a chair.

He sat quietly down opposite me, and, weary as I was, I was conscious of his keen eyes upon me.

"We heard from Miss Holladay this morning," I remarked, unconsciously answering their question.

He did not reply for a moment, but I had closed my eyes again, and I was too tired to open them and look at him.

"Ah," he said, in a voice a little hoarse; "and she is well?"

"No; she's disappeared."

"You mean——"

"I mean she's run away," I said, waking up a little.

"And she has informed you——"

"Oh, no; we've just found it out. She's been gone ten days."

"And you are going to search for her?" he questioned carelessly, after another pause.

"Yes—I'll begin in the morning."

Again there was a moment's silence.

"Ah!" he said, with a curious intensity. "Ah."

Then he arose and left me to tumble incontinently into bed.

### CHAPTER XI: I Unmask My Enemy

Tired Nature asserted herself and took the full twelve hours. But I felt like another man when I left the house next morning, and I was eager to grapple anew with the mystery. I found two reports awaiting me at the office: Mr. Royce had passed a good night and was better; the clerks who had spent the afternoon before in visiting the stables had as yet discovered nothing, and were continuing their search.

I looked up a time-card of the Long Island Railroad, and found that Miss Holladay's coachman could not reach the city until 9.30. So I put on my hat again, sought a secluded table at Wallack's, and over a cigar and stein of bock, drew up a résumé of the case—to clear the atmosphere, as it were. It ran something like this:

March 13, Thursday—Holladay found murdered; daughter drives to Washington Square.

March 14, Friday—Coroner's inquest; Miss Holladay released; mysterious note received.

March 16, Sunday—Holladay buried.

March 18, Tuesday—Will opened and probated.

March 28, Friday—Miss Holladay returns from drive, bringing new maid with her and discharges old one.

March 29, Saturday—Gives orders to open summer house.

April 1, Tuesday—Asks for $100,000.

April 2, Wednesday—Gets it.

April 3, Thursday—Leaves home, ostensibly for Belair, in company with new maid.

April 14, Monday—Butler reports her disappearance; Royce taken ill; I begin my search.

There I stopped. The last entry brought me up to date—there was nothing more to add. But it seemed impossible that all the developments of this mystery should have taken only a month. For years, as it seemed to me, I had thought of nothing else.

I looked over the schedule again carefully. There was only one opening that I could see where it was possible to begin work with the hope of accomplishing anything. That was in the very first entry. Miss Holladay had driven to Washington Square; she had, I felt certain, visited her sister; I must discover the lodging of this woman. Perhaps I should also discover Frances Holladay there. In any event, I should have a new point to work from.

The police had been over the ground, I knew; they had exhausted every resource in the effort to locate Mr. Holladay's mysterious visitor, and had found not a trace of her. But that fact did not discourage me; for I hoped to start my search with information which the police had not possessed. Brooks, the coachman, should be able to tell me——

Recalled suddenly to remembrance of him, I looked at my watch and saw that it was past his hour. I was pleased to find him awaiting me when I opened the office door three minutes later. I had only a few questions to ask him.

"When your mistress left the carriage the day you drove her to Washington Square, did you notice which street she took after she left the square?"

"Yes, sir; she went on down West Broadway."

"On which side?"

"Th' left-hand side, sir; th' east side."

"She must have crossed the street to get to that side."

"Yes, sir; she did. I noticed pertic'lar, for I thought it funny she shouldn't 've let me drive her on down th' street to wherever she was goin'. It's a dirty place along there, sir."

"Yes, I know. When you drove her out on the 28th—the day she brought back the maid—where did she go?"

"To Washington Square again, sir."

"And left you waiting for her?"

"Yes, sir; just th' same."

"And went down the same street?"

"Yes, sir; crossed to th' east side just th' same as th' time before."

"How long was she gone?"

"Over an hour, sir; an hour an' a half, I should say."

"Did you notice anything unusual in her appearance when she came back?"

"No, sir; she was wearin' a heavy veil. She had th' other woman with her, an' she just said 'Home!' in a kind o' hoarse voice, as I helped them into th' carriage."

That was all that he could tell me, and yet I felt that it would help me greatly. In the first place, it narrowed my investigations to the district lying to the east of West Broadway, and I knew that the French quarter extended only a block or two in that direction. And again, it gave me a point to insist on in my inquiries—I knew the date upon which the mysterious woman had left her lodging. Or, at least, I knew that it must be one of two dates. The lodging had been vacated, then, either on the twenty-eighth of March or the third of April. As a last resource, I had the photograph. I was ready to begin my search, and dismissed Brooks, warning him to say nothing to anyone about the mystery.

As I passed out the door to the pavement, I happened to glance across the way, and there, in the crowd of brokers which always lines the street, I perceived Martigny. He was listening intently to one of the brokers, who was talking earnestly in his ear—telling him how to make his fortune, I suppose—and did not see me. For an instant, I was tempted to cross to him, and get him out of danger. Then I smiled at the absurdity of the thought. It would take a clever man to fleece Martigny, and I recalled his strong face, his masterful air—he was no fool, no lamb ready for the shears. He was perfectly able to look out for himself—to wield the shears with power and effect, if need be.

I turned west toward Broadway, still, I suppose, thinking of him subconsciously: for a few moments later, some irresistible impulse caused me to glance around. And there he was, walking after me, on the opposite side of the street! Then, in a flash, I understood. He was following me!

It is difficult to describe the shock that ran through me, that left me numbed and helpless. For an instant, I stumbled on, half-dazed; then, gradually, my self-control came back, and with it a certain fierce joy, a hot exultation. Here, at last, was something definite, tangible, a clew ready to my hand, if only I were clever enough to follow it up; a ray of light in the darkness! I could feel my cheeks burning, and my heart leaping at the thought!

But what had been his part in the affair? For a moment, I groped blindly in the dark, but only for a moment. Whatever his share in the tragedy, he had plainly been left behind to watch us; to make sure that we did not follow the fugitives; to warn them in case of danger. I understood, now, his solicitude for Miss Holladay—"in her I take such an interest!" It was important that he should know the moment we discovered her absence. And he had known; he knew that I was even at this moment commencing the search for her. My cheeks reddened at the thought of my indiscreetness; yet he was a man to command confidence. Who would have suspected him? And an old proverb which he had repeated one evening, flashed through my mind:

"Folle est la brebis qui au loup se confesse."

"Silly is the sheep who to the wolf herself confesses," I had translated it, with that painful literalness characteristic of the beginner. Well, I had been the sheep, and silly enough, Heaven knows!

I had reached Broadway, and at the corner I paused to look at a display of men's furnishings in a window. Far down the street, on the other side, almost lost in the hurrying crowd, Martigny was buying a paper of a newsboy. He shook it out and looked quickly up and down its columns, like a man who is searching for some special item of news. Perhaps he was a speculator; perhaps, after all, I was deceiving myself in imagining that he was following me. I had no proof of it; it was the most natural thing in the world that he should be in this part of the town. I must test the theory before accepting it. It was time I grew wary of theories.

I entered the store, and spent ten minutes looking at some neckties. When I came out again, Martigny was just getting down from a bootblack's chair across the street. His back was toward me, and I watched him get out his little purse and drop a dime into the bootblack's hand. I went on up Broadway, loitering sometimes, sometimes walking straight ahead; always, away behind me, lost in the crowd, was my pursuer. It could no longer be doubted. He was really following me, though he did it so adroitly, with such consummate cunning, that I should never have seen him, never have suspected him, but for that fortunate intuition at the start.

A hundred plans flashed through my brain. I had this advantage: he could not know that I suspected him. If I could only overmaster him in cunning, wrest his secret from him—and then, as I remembered the strong face, the piercing eyes, the perfect self-control, I realized how little possible it was that I could accomplish this. He was my superior in diplomacy and deceit; he would not pause, now, at any means to assure the success of his plot.

Yes, I could doubt no longer that there was a plot, whose depths I had not before even suspected; and I drew back from the thought with a little shiver. What was the plot? What intricate, dreadful crime was this which he was planning? The murder of the father, then, had been only the first step. The abduction of Frances Holladay was the second. What would the third be? How could we prevent his taking it? Suppose we should be unsuccessful? And, candidly, what chance of success could we have, fighting in the dark against this accomplished scoundrel? He had the threads all in his fingers, he controlled the situation; we were struggling blindly, snarled in a net of mystery from which there seemed no escaping. My imagination clothed him with superhuman attributes. For a moment a wild desire possessed me to turn upon him, to confront him, to accuse him, to confound him with the very certainty of my knowledge, to surprise his secret, to trample him down!

But the frenzy passed. No, he must not discover that I suspected him; I must not yield up that advantage. I might yet surprise him, mislead him, set a trap for him, get him to say more than he wished to say. That battle of wits would come later on—this very night, perhaps—but for the moment, I could do nothing better than carry out my first plan. Yet, he must not suspect the direction of my search—I must throw him off the track. Why, this was, for all the world, just like the penny-dreadfuls of my boyhood—and I smiled at the thought that I had become an actor in a drama fitted for a red-and-yellow cover!

My plan was soon made. I crossed Broadway and turned into Cortlandt, sauntering along it until the Elevated loomed just ahead; I heard the roar of an approaching train, and stopped to purchase some fruit at the corner stand. My pursuer was some distance behind, closely inspecting the bric-à-brac in a peddler's cart. The train rumbled into the station, and, starting as though I had just perceived it, I bounded up the stair, slammed my ticket into the chopper, and dived across the platform. The guard at the rear of the train held the gate open for me an instant, and then clanged it shut. We were off with a jerk; as I looked back, I saw Martigny rush out upon the platform. He stood staring after me for an instant; then, with a sudden grasping at his breast, staggered and seemed to fall. A crowd closed about him, the train whisked around a corner, and I could see no more.

But, at any rate, I was well free of him, and I got off at Bleecker Street, walked on to the Square, and began my search. My plan was very simple. Beginning on the east side of West Broadway, it was my intention to stop at every house and inquire whether lodgers were kept. My experience at the first place was a pretty fair sample of all the rest.

A frowsy-headed woman answered my knock.

"You have rooms to let?" I asked.

"Oh, yes, monsieur," she answered, with an expansive grin. "Step zis vay."

We mounted a dirty stair, and she threw open a door with a flourish meant to be impressive. "Zese are ze rooms, monsieur; zey are ver' fine."

I looked around them with simulated interest, smothering my disgust as well as I could.

"How long have they been vacant?" I asked.

"Since only two days, monsieur; as you see, zey are ver' fine rooms."

That settled it. If they had been vacant only two days, I had no further interest in them, and with some excuse I made my way out, glad to escape from that fetid atmosphere of garlic and onions. So I went from house to house; stumbling over dirty children; climbing grimy stairs, catching glimpses of crowded sweat-shops; peering into all sorts of holes called rooms by courtesy; inhaling a hundred stenches in as many minutes; gaining an insight that sickened me into the squalid life of the quarter. Sometimes I began to hope that at last I was on the right track; but further inquiry would prove my mistake. So the morning passed, and the afternoon. I had covered two blocks to no purpose, and at last I turned eastward to Broadway, and took a car downtown to the office. My assistants had reported again—they had met with no better success than I. Mr. Graham noticed my dejected appearance, and spoke a word of comfort.

"I think you're on the right track, Lester," he said. "But you can't hope to do much by yourself—it's too big a job. Wouldn't it be better to employ half a dozen private detectives, and put them under your supervision? You could save yourself this nerve-trying work, and at the same time get over the ground much more rapidly. Besides, experienced men may be able to suggest something that you've overlooked."

I had thought of that—I had wondered if I were making the best possible use of my opportunities—and the suggestion tempted me. But something rose within me—pride, ambition, stubbornness, what you will—and I shook my head, determined to hang on. Besides, I had still before me that battle of wits with Martigny, and I was resolved to make the most of it.

"Let me keep on by myself a day or two longer, sir," I said. "I believe I'll succeed yet. If I don't there will still be time to call in outside help. I fancy I've made a beginning, and I want to see what comes of it."

He shook me kindly by the hand.

"I like your grit," he said approvingly, "and I've every confidence in you—it wasn't lack of confidence that prompted the suggestion. Only don't overdo the thing, and break down as Royce has. He's better, by the way, but the doctor says that he must take a long vacation—a thorough rest."

"I'm glad he's better. I'll be careful," I assented, and left the office.

While I waited for a car I bought a copy of the last edition of the Sun—from force of habit, more than anything; then, settling myself in a seat—still from force of habit—I turned to the financial column and looked it over. There was nothing of special interest there, and I turned back to the general news, glancing carelessly from item to item. Suddenly one caught my eye which brought me up with a shock. The item read:

Shortly after ten o'clock this morning, a man ran up the steps of the Cortlandt Street station of the Sixth Avenue Elevated, in the effort to catch an uptown train just pulling out, and dropped over on the platform with heart disease. An ambulance was called from the Hudson Street Hospital and the man taken there. At noon, it was said he would recover. He was still too weak to talk, but among other things, a card of the Café Jourdain, 54 West Houston Street, was found in his pocket-book. An inquiry there developed the fact that his name is Pierre Bethune, that he is recently from France, and has no relatives in this country.

In a moment I was out of the car and running westward to the Elevated. I felt that I held in my hand the address I needed.

**CHAPTER XII: At the Café Jourdain**

Fifty-four West Houston Street, just three blocks south of Washington Square, was a narrow, four-storied-and-basement building, of gray brick with battered brown-stone trimmings—at one time, perhaps, a fashionable residence, but with its last vestige of glory long since departed. In the basement was a squalid cobbler's shop, and the restaurant occupied the first floor. Dirty lace curtains hung at the windows, screening the interior from the street; but when I mounted the step to the door and entered, I found the place typical of its class. I sat down at one of the little square tables, and ordered a bottle of wine. It was Monsieur Jourdain himself who brought it: a little, fat man, with trousers very tight, and a waistcoat very dazzling. The night trade had not yet begun in earnest, so he was for the moment at leisure, and he consented to drink a glass of wine with me—I had ordered the "supérieur."

"You have lodgings to let, I suppose, on the floors above?" I questioned.

He squinted at me through his glass, trying, with French shrewdness, to read me before answering.

"Why, yes, we have lodgings; still, a man of monsieur's habit would scarcely wish——"

"The habit does not always gauge the purse," I pointed out.

"That is true," he smiled, sipping his wine. "Monsieur then wishes a lodging?"

"I should like to look at yours."

"You understand, monsieur," he explained, "that this is a good quarter, and our rooms are not at all the ordinar' rooms—oh, no, they are quite supérior to that. They are in great demand—we have only one vacant at this moment—in fact, I am not certain that it is yet at liberty. I will call my wife."

She was summoned from behind the counter, where she presided at the money-drawer, and presented to me as Madame Jourdain. I filled a glass for her.

"Monsieur, here, is seeking a lodging," he began. "Is the one on the second floor, back, at our disposal yet, Célie?"

His wife pondered the question a moment, looking at me with sharp little eyes.

"I do not know," she said at last. "We shall have to ask Monsieur Bethune. He said he might again have need of it. He has paid for it until the fifteenth."

My heart leaped at the name. I saw that I must take the bull by the horns—assume a bold front; for if they waited to consult my pursuer, I should never gain the information I was seeking.

"It was through Monsieur Bethune that I secured your address," I said boldly. "He was taken ill this morning; his heart, you know," and I tapped my chest.

They nodded, looking at me, nevertheless, with eyes narrow with suspicion.

"Yes, monsieur, we know," said Jourdain. "The authorities at the hospital at once notified us."

"It is not the first attack," I asserted, with a temerity born of necessity. "He has had others, but none so serious as this."

They nodded sympathetically. Plainly they had been considerably impressed by their lodger.

"So," I continued brazenly, "he knows at last that his condition is very bad, and he wishes to remain at the hospital for some days until he has quite recovered. In the meantime, I am to have the second floor back, which was occupied by the ladies."

I spoke the last word with seeming nonchalance, without the quiver of a lash, though I was inwardly a-quake; for I was risking everything upon it. Then, in an instant I breathed more freely. I saw that I had hit the mark, and that their suspicions were gradually growing less.

"They, of course, are not coming back," I added; "at least, not for a long time; so he has no further use for the room. This is the fourteenth—I can take possession to-morrow."

They exchanged a glance, and Madame Jourdain arose.

"Very well, monsieur," she said. "Will you have the kindness to come and look at the room?"

I followed her up the stair, giddy at my good fortune. She opened a door and lighted a gas-jet against the wall.

"I am sure you will like the apartment, monsieur," she said. "You see, it is a very large one and most comfortable."

It was, indeed, of good size and well furnished. The bed was in a kind of alcove, and beyond it was a bath—unlooked-for luxury! One thing, however, struck me as peculiar. The windows were closed by heavy shutters, which were barred upon the inside, and the bars were secured in place by padlocks.

"I shall want to open the windows," I remarked. "Do you always keep them barred?"

She hesitated a moment, looking a little embarrassed.

"You see, monsieur, it is this way," she explained, at last. "Monsieur Bethune himself had the locks put on; for he feared that his poor sister would throw herself down into the court-yard, which is paved with stone, and where she would certainly have been killed. She was very bad some days, poor dear. I was most glad when they took her away; for the thought of her made me nervous. I will in the morning open the windows, and air the room well for you."

"That will do nicely," I assented, as carelessly as I could. I knew that I had chanced upon a new development, though I could not in the least guess its bearing. "What do you ask for the apartment?"

"Ten dollars the week, monsieur," she answered, eying me narrowly.

I knew it was not worth so much, and, remembering my character, repressed my first inclination to close the bargain.

"That is a good deal," I said hesitatingly. "Haven't you a cheaper room, Madame Jourdain?"

"This is the only one we have now vacant, monsieur," she assured me.

I turned back toward the door with a little sigh.

"I fear I can't take it," I said.

"Monsieur does not understand," she protested. "That price, of course, includes breakfast."

"And dinner?"

She hesitated, eying me again.

"For one dollar additional it shall include dinner."

"Done, madame!" I cried. "I pay you for a week in advance," and I suited the action to the word. "Only," I added, "be sure to air the room well to-morrow—it seems very close. Still,

Bethune was right to make sure that his sister could not harm herself."

"Yes," she nodded, placing the money carefully in an old purse, with the true miserly light in her eyes. "Yes—she broke down most sudden—it was the departure of her mother, you know, monsieur."

I nodded thoughtfully.

"When they first came, six weeks ago, she was quite well. Then her mother a position of some sort secured and went away; she never left her room after that, just sat there and cried, or rattled at the doors and windows. Her brother was heartbroken about her—no one else would he permit to attend her. But I hope that she is well now, poor child, for she is again with her mother."

"Her mother came after her?" I asked.

"Oh, yes; ten days ago, and together they drove away. By this time, they are again in the good France."

I pretended to be inspecting a wardrobe, for I felt sure my face would betray me. At a flash, I saw the whole story. There was nothing more Madame Jourdain could tell me.

"Yes," I repeated, steadying my voice, "the good France."

"Monsieur Bethune has himself been absent for a week," she added, "on affairs of business. He was not certain that he would return, but he paid us to the fifteenth."

I nodded. "Yes: to-morrow—I will take possession then."

"Very well, monsieur," she assented; "I will have it in readiness."

For an instant, I hesitated. Should I use the photograph? Was it necessary? How explain my possession of it? Did I not already know all that Madame Jourdain could tell me? I turned to the stair.

"Then I must be going," I said; "I have some business affairs to arrange," and we went down together.

The place was filling with a motley crowd of diners, but I paused only to exchange a nod with Monsieur Jourdain, and then hurried away. The fugitives had taken the French line, of course, and I hastened on to the foot of Morton Street, where the French line pier is. A ship was being loaded for the voyage out, and the pier was still open. A clerk directed me to the sailing schedule, and a glance at it confirmed my guess. At ten o'clock on the morning of Thursday, April 3d, La Savoie had sailed for Havre.

"May I see La Savoie's passenger list?" I asked.

"Certainly, sir," and he produced it.

I did not, of course, expect to find Miss Holladay entered upon it, yet I felt that a study of it might be repaid; and I was not mistaken. A Mrs. G. R. Folsom and two daughters had occupied the cabine de luxe, 436, 438, 440; on the company's list, which had been given me, I saw bracketed after the name of the youngest daughter the single word "invalid."

"La Lorraine sails day after to-morrow, I believe?" I asked.

"Yes, sir."

"And is she full?"

"No, sir; it is a little early in the season yet," and he got down the list of staterooms, showing me which were vacant. I selected an outside double one, and deposited half the fare, in order to reserve it.

There was nothing more to be done that night, for a glance at my watch showed me the lateness of the hour. As I emerged from the pier, I suddenly found myself very weary and very hungry, so I called a cab and was driven direct to my rooms. A bath and dinner set me up again, and finally I settled down with my pipe to arrange the events of the day.

Certainly I had progressed. I had undoubtedly got on the track of the fugitives; I had found out all that I could reasonably have hoped to find out. And yet my exultation was short-lived. Admitted that I was on their track, how much nearer success had I got? I knew that they had sailed for France, but for what part of France? They would disembark at Havre—how was I, reaching Havre, two weeks later, to discover which direction they had taken? Suppose they had gone to Paris, as seemed most probable, how could I ever hope to find them there? Even if I did find them, would I be in time to checkmate Martigny?

For a time, I paused, appalled at the magnitude of the task that lay before me—in all France, to find three people! But, after all, it might not be so great. Most probably, these women were from one of the towns Holladay and his wife had visited during their stay in France. Which towns they were, I, of course, had no means of knowing; yet I felt certain that some means of discovering them would present itself. That must be my work for the morrow.

A half-hour passed, and I sat lost in speculation, watching the blue smoke curling upward, striving vainly to penetrate the mystery. For I was as far as ever from a solution of it. Who were these people? What was their aim? How had they managed to win Miss Holladay over to their side; to persuade her to accompany them; to flee from her friends—above all, from our junior partner? How had they caused her change of attitude toward him? Or had they really abducted her? Was there really danger of foul play—danger that she would fall a victim, as well as her father? Who was Martigny? And, above all, what was the plot? What did he hope to gain? What was he striving for? What was this great stake, for which he risked so much?

To these questions I could find no reasonable answer; I was still groping aimlessly in the dark; and at last in sheer confusion, I put down my pipe, turned out the light, and went to bed.

## CHAPTER XIII: En Voyage

Mr. Graham's congratulations next morning quite overwhelmed me.

"I never expected such complete and speedy success, Mr. Lester," he said warmly. "You've done splendid work."

I pointed out to him that, after all, my success was purely the result of accident. Had I been really clever, I should have instantly suspected what that sudden seizure on the station platform meant, I should have hurried back to the scene, and followed Martigny—as I still called him in my thoughts—to the hospital, on the chance of securing his first address. Instead of which, if chance had not befriended me, I should have been as far as ever from a solution of the mystery. I trembled to think upon what a slender thread my victory had hung.

But my chief would not listen; he declared that a man must be judged by his achievements, and that he judged me by mine.

"Let us find out how our friend is," I said at last; so the hospital was called up. We were informed that the patient was stronger, but would not be able to leave his bed for two or three days.

"The Jourdains may tell him of my call," I said. "They'll suspect something when I don't return to-day—yet they may wait for me a day or two longer—they have my money—and one day is all I want. It's just possible that they may keep silent altogether. They've nothing to gain by speaking—it's plain that they're not in the conspiracy. Anyway, to-morrow I'll be out of reach."

Mr. Graham nodded.

"Yes—that's plainly the next step. You must follow them to France—but where in France will you look for them? I didn't think of that before. Why, the search is just beginning! I thought it impossible to accomplish what you have accomplished, but that seems easy, now, beside this new problem."

"Yes," I assented; "still, it may not be so hard as it looks. We must try to find out where the women have gone, and I believe Rogers can help us. My theory is that they're from one of the towns which the Holladays visited when they were abroad, and Mr. Holladay must have kept in touch with his office, more or less, during that time."

My chief sprang up and seized his hat.

"The very thing!" he cried. "There's no luck about that bit of reasoning, Mr. Lester. Come, I'll go with you."

"Only," I added, as we went down together, "I very much fear that the search will lead to Paris, for Martigny is undoubtedly a Parisian."

"And to find a person in Paris...."

I did not answer: I only shut my teeth together, and told myself for the hundredth time that I must not fail.

Rogers had been carrying on the routine work of the business since his employer's death, and was supervising the settlement of accounts, and the thousand and one details which must be attended to before the business could be closed up. We found him in the private office, and stated our errand without delay.

"Yes," he said, "Mr. Holladay kept in touch with the office, of course. Let me see—what was the date?"

"Let us look for the first six months of 1876," I suggested.

He got down the file covering that period, and ran through the letters.

"Yes, here they are," he said after a moment. "In January, he writes from Nice, where they seem to have remained during February and March. About the middle of April, they started north—here's a letter dated Paris, April 19th—and from Paris they went to a place called Etretat. They remained there through May, June, and July. That is all the time covered by this file. Shall I get another?"

"No," I answered; "but I wish you'd make an abstract of Mr. Holladay's whereabouts during the whole time he was abroad, and send it to our office not later than this afternoon."

"Very well, sir," he said, and we left the room.

"But why didn't you let him go farther?" asked Mr. Graham, as we left the building.

"Because I think I've found the place, sir," I answered. "Did you notice—the time they stayed at Etretat covers the period of Miss Holladay's birth, with which, I'm convinced, these people were in some way concerned. We must look up Etretat."

A map at the office showed us that it was a little fishing hamlet and seaside resort on the shore of the English Channel, not far north of Havre.

"My theory is," I said, "that when the time of her confinement approached, Mr. Holladay brought his wife to Paris to secure the services of an experienced physician, perhaps; or perhaps a nurse, or linen, or all of them. That done, they proceeded to Etretat, which they may have visited before, and knew for a quiet place, with a bracing atmosphere and good climate—just such a place as they would naturally desire. Here, the daughter was born, and here, I am convinced, we shall find the key to the mystery, though I'm very far from guessing what that key is. But I have a premonition—you may smile if you wish—that I'll find the clew I'm seeking at Etretat. The name has somehow struck an answering chord in me."

The words, as I recall them now, seem more than a little foolish and self-assured; yet, in light of the result—well, at any rate, my chief showed no disposition to smile, but sat for some moments in deep thought.

"I don't doubt that you're right, Mr. Lester," he said at last. "At any rate, I'm ready to trust your experience—since I have absolutely none in this kind of work. I don't need to say that I have every confidence in you. I'll have a letter of credit prepared at once, so that you may not want for money—shall we say five thousand to start with?"

I stammered that I was certain that would be more than enough, but he silenced me with a gesture.

"You'll find foreign travel more expensive than you think," he said. "It may be, too, that you'll find that money will help you materially with your investigations. I want you to have all you may need—don't spare it. When you need more don't hesitate to draw on us."

I thanked him and was about to take my leave, for I had some packing to do and some private business to arrange, when a message came from Doctor Jenkinson. Mr. Graham smiled as he read it.

"Royce is better," he said; "much better. He's asking for you, and Jenkinson seems to think you'd better go to him, especially if you can bring good news."

"Just the thing!" I cried. "I must go to bid him good-by, in any event," and half an hour later I was admitted to our junior's room. He was lying back in a big chair, and seemed pale and weak, but he flushed up when he saw me, and held out his hand eagerly.

"I couldn't wait any longer, Lester," he began. "It seems an age since I've seen you. I'd have sent for you before this, but I knew that you were working."

"Yes," I smiled; "I was working."

"Sit down and tell me about it," he commanded. "All about it—every detail."

The door opened as he spoke, and Dr. Jenkinson came in.

"Doctor," I queried, "how far is it safe to indulge this sick man? He wants me to tell him a story."

"Is it a good story?" asked the doctor.

"Why, yes; fairly good."

"Then tell it. May I stay?"

"Certainly," said Mr. Royce and I together, and the doctor drew up a chair.

So I recounted, as briefly as I could, the events of the past two days, and the happy accident which had given me the address I sought. Mr. Royce's face was beaming when I ended.

"And you start for France to-morrow?" he asked.

"To-morrow morning—the boat sails at ten o'clock."

"Well, I'm going with you!" he cried.

"Why," I stammered, startled by his vehemence, "are you strong enough? I'd be mighty glad to have you, but do you think you ought? How about it, doctor?"

Jenkinson was smiling with half-shut eyes.

"It's not a bad idea," he said. "He needs rest and quiet more than anything else, and he's bound to get a week of that on the water, which is more than he'll do here. I can't keep that brain of his still, wherever he is. He'd worry here, and with you he'll be contented. Besides," he added, "he ought to be along: for I believe the expedition is going to be successful!"

I believed so, too; but I recognized in Jenkinson's words that fine optimism which had done so much to make him the great doctor he was. I shook our junior's hand again in the joy of having him with me. As for him, he seemed quite transformed, and Jenkinson gazed at him with a look of quiet pleasure.

"You'll have to pack," I said. "Will you need my help?"

"No; nurse can do it, with the doctor here to help us out," he laughed. "You've your own packing to do, and odds and ends to look after. Besides, neither of us will need much luggage. Don't forget to reserve the other berth in that stateroom for me."

"No," I said, and rose. "I'll come for you in the morning."

"All right; I'll be ready."

The doctor followed me out to give me a word of caution. Mr. Royce was still far from well; he must not over-exert himself; he must be kept cheerful and hopeful, if possible; above all, he was not to worry; quiet and sea air would do the rest.

I hurried back to the office to make my final report to Mr. Graham, and to get the abstract which Rogers had promised to have ready, and which was awaiting me on my desk. Our worthy senior was genuinely pleased when he learned that his junior was going with me, though our absence would mean a vast deal of extra work for himself. The canvass of the city stables had been completed without result, but I suspected now that Martigny himself had hired the carriage, and had, perhaps, even acted as driver—such an easy and obvious way to baffle our pursuit would hardly have escaped him.

I finished up some odds and ends of work which I had left undone, and finally bade Mr. Graham good-by, and started for my rooms. My packing was soon finished, and I sat down for a final smoke and review of the situation.

There was one development of the day before which quite baffled me. I had proved that there were, indeed, two women, and I believed them to be mother and daughter, but I could not in the least understand why the younger one had so completely broken down after the departure of the elder with Miss Holladay. I looked at this point from every side, but could find no reasonable explanation of it. It might be, indeed, that the younger one was beginning already to repent her share in the conspiracy—there could be no question that it was she who had struck down Holladay in his office—that she had even refused to go farther in the plot, and that her companions had found it necessary to restrain her; but this seemed to me too exceedingly improbable to believe. And, as I went over the ground again, I found myself beginning more and more to doubt the truth of Godfrey's theory, though I could formulate none to take its place; I became lost in a maze of conjecture, and, at last, I gave it up and went to bed.

I called for Mr. Royce, as we had agreed, and together we drove down to Morton Street. He, too, had limited his baggage to a single small trunk. We secured a deck-hand to take them into our stateroom, and, after seeing them disposed of, went out on deck to watch the last preparations for departure. The pier was in that state of hurly-burly which may be witnessed only at the sailing of a transatlantic liner. The last of the freight was being got aboard with frantic haste; the boat and pier were crowded with people who had come to bid their friends good-by; two tugs were puffing noisily alongside, ready to pull us out into the stream. My companion appeared quite strong, and seemed to enjoy the bustle and hubbub as much as I did. He flushed with pleasure, as he caught sight of our senior pushing his way toward us.

"Why, this is kind of you, sir!" he cried, grasping his hand. "I know what the work of the office must be, with both of us deserting you this way."

"Tut, tut!" and Mr. Graham smiled at us. "You deserve a vacation, don't you? I couldn't let you go without telling you good-by. Besides," he added, "I learned just this morning that two very dear friends of mine are taking this boat—Mrs. Kemball and her daughter—the widow of Jim Kemball, you know."

Mr. Royce nodded. I, too, recalled the name—Jim Kemball had been one of the best men at the

New York bar twenty years before, and must inevitably have made a great name for himself but for his untimely death. I had heard a hundred stories of him.

"Well, I want you to meet them," continued Mr. Graham, looking about in all directions. "Ah, here they are!" and he dragged his partner away toward the bow of the boat. I saw him bowing before a gray-haired little lady, and a younger and taller one whose back was toward me. They laughed together for a moment, then the last bell rang, and the ship's officers began to clear the boat. I turned back to the pier, but was brought round an instant later by Mr. Graham's voice.

"My dear Lester," he cried, "I thought we'd lost you. I want to introduce you to Mrs. Kemball and her daughter, who are to be your fellow voyagers. Mr. Lester's a very ingenious young man," he added. "Make him amuse you!" and he hastened away to catch the gang-plank before it should be pulled in.

I bowed to Mrs. Kemball, thinking to myself that I had never seen a sweeter, pleasanter face. Then I found myself looking into a pair of blue eyes that fairly took my breath away.

"We'll not neglect Mr. Graham's advice," said a merry voice. "So prepare for your fate, Mr. Lester!"

There was a hoarse shouting at the gang-way behind me, and the eyes looked past me, over my shoulder.

"See," she said; "there's one poor fellow who has just made it."

I turned and looked toward the gang-plank. One end had been cast loose, but two deck-hands were assisting another man to mount it. He seemed weak and helpless, and they supported him on either side. An involuntary cry rose to my lips as I looked at him, but I choked it back. For it was Martigny, risen from his bed to follow us!

## CHAPTER XIV: I Prove a Bad Sentinel

I watched him with a kind of fascination until he disappeared through the door of the cabin. I could guess what it had cost him to drag himself from his bed, what agony of apprehension must have been upon him to make him take the risk. The Jourdains, puzzled at my not returning, unable to keep silence, suspecting, perhaps, some plot against themselves, had doubtless gone to the hospital and told him of my appearance—there had been no way for me to guard against that. He had easily guessed the rest. He had only to consult the passenger list to assure himself that Mr. Royce and I were aboard. And he was following us, hoping—what? What could a man in his condition hope to accomplish? What need was there for us to fear him? And yet, there was something about him—something in the atmosphere of the man—that almost terrified me.

I came back to earth to find that Royce and Mrs. Kemball had drifted away together, and that my companion was regarding me from under half-closed lids with a little smile of amusement.

"So you're awake again, Mr. Lester?" she asked. "Do you often suffer attacks of that sort?"

"Pardon me," I stammered. "The fact is, I—I——"

"You looked quite dismayed," she continued relentlessly. "You seemed positively horror-stricken. I saw nothing formidable about him."

"No; you don't know him!" I retorted, and stopped, lest I should say too much.

She was smiling broadly, now; an adorable smile that wrinkled up the corners of her eyes, and gave me a glimpse of little white teeth.

"I think we'd better sit down," she said.

"Your knees seem to be still somewhat shaky. Mother and Mr. Royce have deserted us."

So we sought a seat near the stern, where we could watch the city sink gradually away in the distance, as the great boat glided smoothly out into the bay, her engines starting on the rhythm which was to continue ceaselessly until the voyage ended. I confess frankly I was worried. I had not thought for a moment that Martigny would have the temerity to board the same boat with us—yet it was not so wonderful after all, since he could not guess that I suspected him, that I knew him and Bethune to be the same person. That was my great advantage. In any event, we were in no danger from him; he was probably following us only that he might warn his confederates, should we seem likely to discover them. Certainly they were in no present danger of discovery, and perhaps might never be. But his following us, his disregard of the grave danger to himself, gave me a new measure of his savage determination to baffle us; I found myself more and more beginning to fear him. My fancy cast about him a sinister cloud, from the depths of which he peered out at us, grim, livid, threatening.

Should I inform Mr. Royce of this new development? I asked myself; then I remembered the doctor's words. He must have rest and quiet during the coming week; he must be free from worry.

"I trust that I'm not in the way, Mr. Lester?" inquired a low, provoking voice at my side, and I awoke to the fact that I had again been guilty of forgetting my companion.

"Miss Kemball," I began desperately, "let me confess that I'm in an exceedingly vexatious situation. The fact that I can't ask advice makes it worse."

"You can't ask even Mr. Royce?" she queried, with raised brows.

"He least of all. You see, he's just recovering from a severe nervous breakdown—he must have quiet—that's one reason he's taking this voyage."

"I see," she nodded.

I glanced at her again—at the open, candid eyes, the forceful mouth and chin—and I took a sudden resolution.

"Miss Kemball," I said, "I'm going to ask your help—that is, if I may."

"Of course you may."

"Well, then, that man who came on board last is the inveterate enemy of both Mr. Royce and myself. We're trying to unearth a particularly atrocious piece of villainy in which he's concerned. I have reason to believe him capable of anything, and a very fiend of cleverness. I don't know what he may plot against us, but I'm certain he'll plot something. Mr. Royce doesn't even know him by sight, and shouldn't be worried; but, unless he's forewarned, he may walk right into danger. I want you to help me keep an eye on him—to help me keep him out of danger. If we look after him closely enough, I shan't need to warn him. Will you help me?"

Her eyes were dancing as she looked up at me.

"Why, certainly!" she cried. "So we're to have a mystery—just we two!"

"Just we two!" I assented with a quickened pulse.

She looked at me doubtfully for a moment.

"I must remember Mr. Graham's warning," she said. "You haven't invented this astonishing story just to entertain me, Mr. Lester?"

"On my word, no," I responded, a little bitterly. "I only wish I had!"

"There," she said contritely; "I shouldn't have doubted! Forgive me, Mr. Lester. Only it seemed so fantastic—so improbable——"

"It is fantastic," I assented, "but, unfortunately, it is true. We must keep an eye on Monsieur Martigny or Bethune."

"Which is his real name?"

"Those are the only ones I know, but I doubt if either is the true one."

Royce and Mrs. Kemball joined us a moment later, and we sat watching the low, distant Long Island shore until the gong summoned us to lunch. A word to the steward had secured us one of the small tables in an alcove at the side—Mrs. Kemball and her daughter surrendered the grandeurs of the captain's table willingly, even gladly, to minister to us—and the meal was a merry one, Mr. Royce seeming in such spirits that I was more than ever determined not to disturb him with the knowledge of Martigny's presence.

As the moments passed, my fears seemed more and more uncalled for. It was quite possible, I told myself, that I had been making a bogy of my own imaginings. The Frenchman did not appear in the saloon, and, afterwards, an inquiry of the ship's doctor developed the fact that he was seriously ill, and quite unable to leave his state room.

So afternoon and evening passed. There were others on board who claimed their share of the charming Mrs. Kemball and her daughter. Mr. Royce knew a few of them, too, and introduced me to them, but I found their talk somehow flat and savorless. I fancied that my companion looked slightly wearied, too, and at last we stole away to our deck chairs, where we sat for an hour or more looking out across the dancing waves, listening to the splash of the boat as she rose and fell over them. He was thinking, no doubt, of a certain dark beauty, whose caprices there was no explaining. As for me—well, I had suddenly developed a sturdy preference for blue eyes.

I may as well confess at once that I was seasick. It came next morning, ten minutes after I had left my berth—not a violent sickness, but a faintness and giddiness that made me long for my berth again. But Mr. Royce would not hear of it. He got me out on deck and into my chair, with the fresh breeze blowing full in my face. There was a long line of chairs drawn up there, and from the faces of most of their occupants, I judged they were far more miserable than I. At the end of an hour, thanks to this treatment, I felt almost well again, and could devour with some appetite the luncheon which Mr. Royce ordered for me.

After a while the doctor came down the line and looked at each of us, stopping for a moment's chat. The more serious cases were below, and all that any of us needed was a little encouragement.

"Won't you sit down a minute, doctor?" I asked, when he came to me, and motioned to Mr. Royce's chair.

"Why, you're not sick!" he protested, laughing, but he dropped into the vacant place.

"It wasn't about myself I wanted to talk," I said. "How's your other patient—the one who came aboard last?"

His face sobered in an instant.

"Martigny is his name," he said, "and he's in very bad shape. He must have been desperately anxious to get back to France. Why, he might have dropped over dead there on the gang-plank."

"It's a disease of the heart?"

"Yes—far advanced. He can't get well, of course, but he may live on indefinitely, if he's careful."

"He's still confined to his bed?"

"Oh, yes—he won't leave it during the voyage, if he takes my advice. He's got to give his heart just as little work as possible, or it'll throw up the job altogether. He has mighty little margin to go on."

I turned the talk to other things, and in a few moments he went on along his rounds. But I was not long alone, for I saw Miss Kemball coming toward me, looking a very Diana, wind-blown and rosy-cheeked.

"So mal-de-mer has laid its hand on you, too, Mr. Lester!" she cried.

"Only a finger," I said. "But a finger is enough. Won't you take pity on a poor landsman and talk to him?"

"But that's reversing our positions!" she protested, sitting down, nevertheless, to my great satisfaction. "It was you who were to be the entertainer! Is our Mephisto abroad yet?" she asked, in a lower tone. "I, too, am feeling his fascination—I long for another glimpse of him."

"Mephisto is still wrestling with his heart, which, it seems, is scarcely able to furnish the blood necessary to keep him going. The doctor tells me that he'll probably spend the voyage abed."

"So there'll be nothing for us to do, after all! Do you know, Mr. Lester, I was longing to become a female Lecoq!"

"Perhaps you may still have the chance," I said gloomily. "I doubt very much whether Mephisto will consent to remain inactive. He doesn't look to be that sort."

She clapped her hands, and nodded a laughing recognition to one of the passing promenaders.

"You're going to Paris, aren't you, Miss Kemball?" I asked.

"To Paris—yes. You too? You must be, since you're going to France."

"We go first to Etretat," I said, and stopped, as she leaned, laughing, back in her chair. "Why, what's wrong with that?" I demanded, in some astonishment.

"Wrong? Oh, nothing. Etretat's a most delightful place—only it recalled to me an amusing memory of how my mother was one day scandalized there by some actresses who were bathing. It's the prettiest little fishing-village, with the finest cliffs I ever saw. But it's hardly the season for Etretat—the actresses have not yet arrived. You'll find it dull."

"We will not stay there long," I said. "But tell me about it. I should like to know."

"Etretat," said my companion, "is rather a bohemian resort. Alphonse Karr discovered it somewhere back in the dark ages, and advertised it—the Etretatians were immensely grateful, and named the main street of the town after him—and since then a lot of artists and theatrical people have built villas there. It has a little beach of gravel where people bathe all day long. When one's tired of bathing, there are the cliffs and the downs, and in the evening there's the casino. You know French, Mr. Lester?"

"Why," I explained, "I was supposed to study it at college. I still remember my 'j'ai, tu a, il a.'"

"You'll remember more when you get to Etretat," she laughed. "You'll have to, or starve."

"Oh, I also know the phrase made immortal by Mark Twain."

"'Avez-vous du vin?'—yes."

"And I think I also have a hazy recollection of the French equivalents for bread and butter and cheese and meat. We shan't starve—besides, I think Mr. Royce can help. He's been to France."

"Of course—and here he comes to claim his chair."

"I won't permit him to claim it if you'll use it a little longer," I protested.

"Oh, but I must be going," and she arose, laughing. "Have I been a satisfactory entertainer?"

"More than satisfactory; I'll accept no other."

"But you won't need any at all, after this morning—I don't really believe you're ill now!"

She nodded to Royce, and moved away without waiting for my answer, which somehow halted on my lips; and so I was left to the rosiest, the most improbable of day dreams.

Saturday, Sunday, and Monday passed, with only such incidents to enliven them as are common to all voyages. But I saw that quiet and sea air were doing their work well with my companion, and that he was steadily regaining his normal health. So I felt more and more at liberty to devote myself to Miss Kemball—in such moments as she would permit me—and I found her fascination increasing in a ratio quite geometrical. Martigny was still abed, and, so the ship's doctor told me, was improving very slowly.

It was Tuesday evening that Mrs. Kemball and her daughter joined us on the promenade, and weary, at last, of Strauss waltzes and Sousa marches, we sauntered away toward the bow of the boat, where the noise from the orchestra could reach us only in far-away snatches. We found a seat in the shadow of the wheel-house, and sat for a long time talking of many things, watching the moonlight across the water. At last we arose to return, and Royce and Mrs. Kemball started on ahead, after a habit they had fallen into, which, now I think of it, I am sure was our junior's doing.

"Two more days, and we'll be at Havre," I said. "I'll be very sorry, Miss Kemball."

"Sorry? I'd never have suspected you of such a fondness for the ocean!"

"Oh, it's not the ocean!" I protested, and—what with the moonlight and the soft night and the opportunity—"the time and the place and the loved one, all together"—would have uttered I know not what folly, had she not sprung suddenly forward with a sharp cry of alarm.

"Mr. Royce!" she cried. "Mother!"

They stopped and turned toward her, just as a heavy spar crashed to the deck before them.

## CHAPTER XV: Two Heads are Better than One

I understood in a flash what had happened, and sprang up the stair to the upper deck, determined to have it out with our enemy, once for all. I searched it over thoroughly, looking in and under the boats and behind funnels and ventilators, but could discover no sign of anyone. When I got back to the promenade, a little crowd had gathered, attracted by the noise of the falling spar, which a dozen members of the crew were busy hoisting back into place.

"I do not see how those lashings could have worked loose," said the officer in charge. "We lashed that extra spar there just before we sailed, and I know it was well fastened."

I took a look at the lashings. They had not been cut, as I expected to find them, but had been untied. Martigny had doubtless worked at them while we sat there talking—he was too clever an artist in crime to do anything so clumsy as to cut the ropes.

"Well, luckily, there's no damage done," observed Mr. Royce, with affected lightness, "though it was a close shave. If Miss Kemball hadn't called to us, the spar would have struck us squarely."

Mrs. Kemball closed her eyes with a giddy little gesture, at the vision the words called up, and the officer frowned in chagrin and perplexity. Just then the captain came up, and the two stepped aside for a consultation in voices so low that only an excited word of French was now and then audible. I turned to Miss Kemball, who was leaning against the rail with white face and eyes large with terror.

"But it was not an accident, Mr. Lester!" she whispered. "I saw a man leaning over the spar—a mere shadowy figure—but I know I could not be mistaken."

I nodded. "I don't doubt it in the least. But don't tell your mother. It will only alarm her needlessly. We'll talk it over in the morning."

She said good-night, and led her mother away toward their stateroom. I went at once in search of the ship's doctor, and met him at the foot of the saloon staircase.

"How is Martigny, doctor?" I asked.

"Worse, I fear," he answered hurriedly. "He has just sent for me."

"Which room has he?"

"He's in 375; an outside room on the upper deck," and he ran on up the stair.

I went forward to the smoking room, and looked over the colored plan of the ship posted there. A moment's inspection of it showed me how easily Martigny had eluded pursuit—he had only to walk twenty feet, open a door, and get into bed again. But, evidently, even that small exertion had been too much for him, and I turned away with the grim thought that perhaps our enemy would kill himself yet.

When I sat down, next morning, beside Miss Kemball, she closed her book, and turned to me with a very determined air.

"Of course, Mr. Lester," she began, "if you think any harm can come from telling me, I don't want you to say a word; but I really think I'm entitled to an explanation."

"So do I," I agreed. "You've proved yourself a better guard than I. I'd forgotten all about

Martigny—I was thinking, well, of something very different—I had no thought of danger."

"Nor had I," she said quickly. "But I chanced to look up and see that dark figure bending over them, and I cried out, really, before I had time to think—involuntarily."

"It was just that which saved them. If you'd stopped to think, it would have been too late."

"Yes—but, oh, I could think afterwards! I'd only to close my eyes, last night, to see him there yet, peering down at us, waiting his opportunity. And then, of course, I puzzled more or less, over the whole thing."

"You shan't puzzle any more," I said, and looked about to make certain that there was no one near. Then, beginning with the death of Hiram Holladay, I laid the case before her, step by step. She listened with clasped hands and intent face, not speaking till I had finished. Then she leaned back in her chair with a long sigh.

"Why, it's horrible!" she breathed. "Horrible and dreadfully puzzling. You haven't told me your explanation yet, Mr. Lester."

"I haven't any explanation," I said helplessly. "I've built up half a dozen theories, but they've all been knocked to pieces, one after the other. I don't know what to think, unless Miss Holladay is a victim of hypnotism or dementia of some kind, and that seems absurd."

"Sometimes she's nice and at other times she's horrid. It recalls 'Dr. Jekyll and Mr. Hyde,' doesn't it?"

"Yes, it does; only, as I say, such an explanation seems absurd."

She sat for a moment with eyes inwardly intent.

"There's one theory which might explain it—part of it. Perhaps it wasn't Miss Holladay at all who returned from Washington Square with the new maid. Perhaps it was the other woman, and the barred windows were really to keep Miss Holladay a prisoner. Think of her there, in that place, with Martigny for her jailer!"

"But she wasn't there!" I protested. "We saw her when we gave her the money. Royce and I saw her—so did Mr. Graham."

"Yes—in a darkened room, with a bandage about her forehead; so hoarse she could scarcely speak. No wonder Mr. Royce hardly knew her!"

I stopped a moment to consider.

"Remember, that would explain something which admits of no other reasonable explanation," went on my companion; "the barred windows and the behavior of the prisoner."

"It would explain that, certainly," I admitted, though, at first thought, the theory did not appeal to me. "You believe, then that Miss Holladay was forcibly abducted?"

"Undoubtedly. If her mind was going to give way at all, it would have done so at once, and not two weeks after the tragedy."

"But if she had brooded over it," I objected.

"She wasn't brooding—at least, she had ceased to brood. You have Mr. Royce's word and the butler's word that she was getting better, brighter, quite like her old self again. Why should she relapse?"

"I don't know," I said helplessly. "The more I reason about it, the more unreasonable it all seems. Besides, that affair last night has upset me so that I can't think clearly. I feel that I was careless—that I wasn't doing my duty."

"I shouldn't worry about it; though, of course," she added a little severely, "you've realized by this time that you alone are to blame for Martigny's presence on the boat."

"But I had to go to the Jourdains'," I protested, "and I couldn't help their going to him—to have asked them not to go would have made them suspect me at once."

"Oh, yes; but, at least, you needn't have sent them. They might not have gone at all—certainly they wouldn't have gone so promptly—if you hadn't sent them."

"Sent them?" I repeated, and stared at her in amazement, doubting if I had heard aright.

"Yes, sent them," she said again, emphatically. "Why do you suppose they went to the hospital so early the next morning?"

"I supposed they had become suspicious of me."

"Nonsense! What possible reason could they have for becoming suspicious of you. On the contrary, it was because they were not suspicious of you, because they wished to please you, to air your room for you; because, in a word, you asked them to go—they went after the key to those padlocks on the window-shutters. Of course, Martigny had it."

For a moment, I was too nonplused to speak; I could only stare at her. Then I found my tongue.

"Well, I was a fool, wasn't I?" I demanded bitterly. "To think that I shouldn't have foreseen that! I was so worked up over my discovery that night that I couldn't think of anything else. Of course, when they asked for the key, the whole story came out."

"I shouldn't blame myself too severely," laughed Miss Kemball, as she looked at my rueful countenance. "I myself think it's rather fortunate that he's on the boat."

"Fortunate? You don't mean that!"

"Precisely that. Suppose the Jourdains hadn't gone to him; he'd have left the hospital anyway in two or three days—he isn't the man to lie inactive when he knew you were searching for the fugitives. He'd have returned, then, to his apartment next to yours; your landlady would have told him that you had sailed for Europe, and he had only to examine this boat's passenger-list to discover your name. So you see there wasn't so much lost, after all."

"But, at any rate," I pointed out, "he would still have been in America. He couldn't have caught us. We'd have had a good start of him."

"He couldn't have caught you, but a cablegram would have passed you in mid-ocean, warning his confederates. If they have time to conceal their prisoner, you'll never find her—your only hope is in catching them unprepared. And there's another reason—since he's on the boat, you've another opportunity—why not go and have a talk with him—that battle of wits you were looking forward to?"

"I'd thought of that," I said; "but I'm afraid I couldn't play the part."

"The part?"

"Of seeming not to suspect him, of being quite frank and open with him, of appearing to tell him all my plans. I'm afraid he'd see through me in the first moment and catch me tripping. It's too great a risk."

"The advantage would be on your side," she pointed out; "you could tell him so many things which he already knows, and which he has no reason to suspect you know he knows—it sounds terribly involved, doesn't it? But you understand?"

"Oh, yes; I understand."

"And then, it would be the natural thing for you to look him up as soon as you learned he was ill. To avoid him will be to confess that you suspect him."

"But his name isn't on the passenger list. If I hadn't happened to see him as he came on board, I'd probably not have known it at all."

"Perhaps he saw you at the same time."

"Then the fat's in the fire," I said. "If he knows I know he's on board, then he also knows that I suspect him; if he doesn't know, why, there's no reason for him to think that I'll find it out, unless he appears in the cabin; which doesn't seem probable."

She sat silent for a moment, looking out across the water.

"Perhaps you're right," she said at last; "there's no use taking any unnecessary risks. The thing appealed to me—I think I should enjoy a half-hour's talk with him, matching my wits against his."

"But yours are brighter than mine," I pointed out. "You've proved it pretty effectually in the last few minutes."

"No I haven't; I've simply shown you that you overlooked one little thing. And I think you're right about the danger of going to Martigny. Our first duty is to Miss Holladay; we must rescue her before he can warn his confederates to place her out of our reach."

The unstudied way in which she said "our" filled me with an unreasoning happiness.

"But why should they bother with a prisoner at all? They didn't shrink from striking down her father?"

"And they may not shrink from striking her down, at a favorable moment," she answered calmly. "It will be easier in France than in New York—they perhaps have the necessary preparations already made—they may be only hesitating—a warning from Martigny may turn the scale."

My hands were trembling at the thought of it. If we should really be too late!

"But I don't believe they'll go to such extremes, Mr. Lester," continued my companion. "I believe you're going to find her and solve the mystery. My theory doesn't solve it, you know; it only makes it deeper. The mystery, after all, is—who are these people?—why did they kill Mr. Holladay?—why have they abducted his daughter?—what is their plot?"

"Yes," I assented; and again I had a moment of confused perplexity, as of a man staring down into a black abyss.

"But after you find her," she asked, "what will you do with her?"

"Do with her? Why, take her home, of course."

"But she'll very probably be broken down, perhaps even on the verge of hysteria. Such an experience would upset any woman, I don't care how robust she may have been. She'll need rest and care. You must bring her to us at Paris, Mr. Lester."

I saw the wisdom of her words, and said so.

"That's very kind of you," I added. "I am sure Mr. Royce will agree—but we have first to find her, Miss Kemball."

I was glad for my own sake, too; the parting of to-morrow would not, then, be a final one. I should see her again. I tried to say something of this, but my tongue faltered and refused to shape the words.

She left me, presently, and for an hour or more I sat there and looked, in every aspect, at the theory she had suggested. Certainly, there was nothing to disprove it; and yet, as she had said, it merely served to deepen the mystery. Who were these people, I asked myself again, who dared to play so bold and desperate a game? The illegitimate daughter might, of course, impersonate Miss Holladay; but who was the elder woman? Her mother? Then the liaison must have taken place in France—her accent was not to be mistaken; but in France Mr. Holladay had been always with his wife. Besides, the younger woman spoke English perfectly. True, she had said only a few words—the hoarseness might have been affected to conceal a difference in voice—but how explain the elder woman's resemblance to Hiram Holladay's daughter? Could they both be illegitimate? But that was nonsense, for Mrs. Holladay had taken her into her life, had loved her——

And Martigny? Who was he? What was his connection with these women? That the crime had been carefully planned I could not doubt; and it had been carried out with surprising skill. There had been no nervous halting at the supreme moments, no hesitation nor drawing back; instead, a coolness of execution almost fiendish, arguing a hardened and practiced hand.

Doubtless it was Martigny who had arranged the plot, who had managed its development. And with what boldness! He had not feared to be present at the inquest; nor even to approach me and discuss the case with me. I tried to recall the details of our talk, impatient that I had paid so little heed to it. He had asked, I remembered, what would happen to Frances Holladay if she were found guilty. He had been anxious, then, to save her. He had—yes, I saw it now!—he had written the note which did save her; he had run the risk of discovery to get her free!

But why?

If I only had a clew; one thread to follow! One ray of light would be enough! Then I could see my way out of this hopeless tangle; I should know how to strike. But to stumble blindly onward in the dark—that might do more harm than good.

Yes, and there was another thing for me to guard against. What was to prevent him, the moment he stepped ashore, wiring to his confederates, warning them, telling them to flee? Or he might wait, watching us, until he saw that they were really in danger. In either event, they must easily escape; Miss Kemball had been right when she pointed out that our only hope was in catching them unprepared. If I could throw him off, deceive him, convince him that there was no danger!

The impulse was too strong to be resisted. In a moment I was on my feet—but, no—to surprise him would be to make him suspect! I called a steward.

"Take this card up to Monsieur Martigny," I said, "in 375, and ask if he is well enough to see me."

As he hurried away, a sudden doubt seized me; horrified at my hardihood, I opened my mouth to call him back. But I did not call: instead, I sank back into my chair and stared out across the water. Had I done well? Was it wise to tempt Providence? Would I prove a match for my enemy? The next half hour would tell. Perhaps he would not see me; he could plead illness; he might be really too ill.

"Monsieur Martigny," said the steward's voice at my elbow, "answers that he will be most pleased to see Monsieur Lester at once."

## CHAPTER XVI: I Beard the Lion

Martigny was lying back in his berth, smoking a cigarette, and, as I entered, he motioned me to a seat on the locker against the wall.

"It was most kind of you to come," he said, with his old smile.

"It was only by accident I learned you were on board," I explained, as I sat down. "You're getting better?"

"I believe so; though this physician is—what you call—an alarmist—most of them are, indeed; the more desperate the illness, the more renowned the cure! Is it not so? He has even forbidden me cigarettes, but I prefer to die than to do without them. Will you not have one?" and he motioned to the pile that lay beside him.

"Thank you," I said, selected one, and lighted it. "Your cigarettes are not to be resisted. But if you are so ill, why did you attempt the voyage? Was it not imprudent?"

"A sudden call of business," he explained airily; "unexpected but—what you call—imperative. Besides, this bed is the same as any other. You see, I have a week of rest."

"The doctor—it was he who mentioned your name to me—it was not on the sailing-list——"

"No." He was looking at me sharply. "I came on board at the last moment—the need was ver' sudden, as I have said. I had not time to engage a stateroom."

"That explains it. Well, the doctor told me that you were bed-fast."

"Yes—since the voyage began I have not left it. I shall not arise until we reach Havre to-morrow."

I watched him as he went through the familiar motion of lighting a second cigarette from the first one. In the half-light of the cabin, I had not at first perceived how ill he looked; now, I saw the dark patches under the eyes, the livid and flabby face, the shaking hand. And for the first time, with a little shock, I realized how near he had been to death.

"But you, Mistair Lester," he was saying, "how does it occur that you also are going to France? I did not know you contemplated——"

"No," I answered calmly, for I had seen that the question was inevitable and I even welcomed it, since it gave me opportunity to get my guns to going. "No; the last time I saw you, I didn't contemplate it, but a good deal has happened since then. Would you care to hear? Are you strong enough to talk?"

Oh, how I relished tantalizing him!

"I should like very exceedingly to hear," he assured me, and shifted his position a little, so that his face was in the shadow. "The beams of light through the shutter make my eyes to hurt," he added.

So he mistrusted himself; so he was not finding the part an easy one, either! The thought gave me new courage, new audacity.

"You may remember," I began, "that I told you once that if I ever went to work on the Holladay case, I'd try first to find the murderess. I succeeded in doing it the very first day."

"Ah!" he breathed. "And after the police had failed! That was, indeed, remarkable. How did you accomplish it?"

"By the merest chance—by great good fortune. I was making a search of the French quarter, house by house, when, on Houston Street, I came to a restaurant, the Café Jourdain. A bottle of supérieur set Jourdain's tongue to wagging; I pretended I wanted a room; he dropped a word, the merest hint; and, in the end, I got the whole story. It seems there was not only one woman, there were two."

"Yes?"

"Yes—and a man whose name was Betuny or Bethune, or something like that. But I didn't pay much attention to him—he doesn't figure in the case. He didn't even go away with the women. The very day I set out on my search, he was picked up on the streets somewhere suffering with apoplexy and taken to a hospital, so nearly dead that it was a question whether he would recover. So he's out of it. The Jourdains told me that the women had sailed for France."

"You will pardon me," said my hearer, "but in what way did you make sure that they were the women you desired?"

"By the younger one's resemblance to Miss Holladay," I answered, lying with a glibness which surprised myself. "The Jourdains maintained that a photograph of Miss Holladay was really one of their lodger."

I heard him draw a deep breath, but he kept his face under admirable control.

"Ah, yes," he said. "That was exceedingly clever. I should never have thought of that. That is worthy of Monsieur Lecoq. And so you follow them to France—but, surely, you have some more—what you call—definite address than that, Mistair Lester!"

I could feel his eyes burning out from the shadows; I was thankful for the cigarette—it helped me to preserve an indifferent countenance.

"No," I said. "It seems rather a wild-goose chase, doesn't it? But you could advise me, Mr. Martigny. Where would it be best for me to search for them?"

He did not answer for a moment, and I took advantage of the opportunity to select a second cigarette and light it. I dared not remain unoccupied; I dared not meet his eyes; I trembled to see that my hand was not wholly steady.

"That," he began slowly, at last, "seems to me a most—ah!—deeficult affair, Mistair Lester. To search for three people through all France—there seems little hope of success. Yet I should think it most likely that they have gone to Paris."

I nodded. "That was my own theory," I agreed. "But to find them in Paris, seems also impossible."

"Not if one uses the police," he said. "It could, most probably, be soon achieved, if you requested the police to assist you."

"But, my dear sir," I protested. "I can't use the police. Miss Holladay, at least, has committed no crime; she has simply chosen to go away without informing us."

"You will permit me to say, then, Mistair Lester," he observed, with just a touch of irony, "that I fail to comprehend your anxiety concerning her."

I felt that I had made a mis-step; that I had need to go carefully.

"It is not quite so simple as that," I explained. "The last time we saw Miss Holladay, she told us that she was ill, and intended to go to her country home for a rest. Instead of going there, she sailed for France, without informing anyone—indeed, doing everything she could to escape detection. That conduct seems so eccentric that we feel in duty bound to investigate it. Besides, two days before she left she received from us a hundred thousand dollars in cash."

I saw him move uneasily on his bed; after all, this advantage of mine was no small one. No wonder he grew restless under this revelation of secrets which were not secrets!

"Ah!" he said softly; and again, "Ah! Yes, that seems peculiar. Yet, perhaps, if you had waited for a letter——"

"Suppose we had waited, and there had been no letter—suppose, in consequence of waiting, we should be too late?"

"Too late? Too late for what, Mistair Lester? What is it you fear for her?"

"I don't know," I answered; "but something—something. At least, we could not assume the responsibility of delay."

"No," he agreed; "perhaps not. You are doubtless quite right to investigate. I wish you success—I wish that I myself might aid you, there is so much of interest in the case to me; but I fear that to be impossible. I must rest—I who have so many affairs calling me, so little desire to rest! Is not the fate ironical?"

And he breathed a sigh, which was doubtless genuine enough.

"Will you go to Paris?" I asked.

"Oh, no; not at once. At Havre I shall meet my agent and transact my affairs with him. Then I shall seek some place of quiet along the coast."

"Yes," I said to myself, with leaping heart, "Etretat!" But I dared not speak the word.

"I shall write to you," he added, "when I have settled. Where do you stay at Paris?"

"We haven't decided yet," I said.

"We?" he repeated.

"Didn't I tell you? Mr. Royce, our junior partner, is with me—he's had a breakdown in health, too, and needed a rest."

"It is no matter where you stay," he said; "I shall write to you at the poste restante. I should like both you and your friend to be my guests before you return to Amer-ric'."

There was a courtesy, a cordiality in his tone which almost disarmed me. Such a finished scoundrel! It seemed a shame that I couldn't be friends with him, for I enjoyed him so thoroughly.

"We shall be glad to accept," I answered, knowing in my heart that the invitation would never be made. "You're very kind."

He waved his hand deprecatingly, then let it fall upon the bed with a gesture of weariness. I recognized the sign of dismissal. I was ready to go; I had accomplished all I could hope to accomplish; if I had not already disarmed his suspicions, I could never do so.

"I am tiring you!" I said, starting up. "How thoughtless of me!"

"No," he protested; "no"; but his voice was almost inaudible.

"I will go," I said. "You must pardon me. I hope you will soon be better," and I closed the door behind me with his murmured thanks in my ears.

It was not till after dinner that I found opportunity to relate to Miss Kemball the details of my talk with Martigny. She listened quietly until I had finished; then she looked at me smilingly.

"Why did you change your mind?" she asked.

"The adventure tempted me—those are your own words. I thought perhaps I might be able to throw Martigny off the track."

"And do you think you succeeded?"

"I don't know," I answered doubtfully. "He may have seen clear through me."

"Oh, I don't believe him superhuman! I believe you succeeded."

"We shall know to-morrow," I suggested.

"Yes—and you must keep up the deception till the last moment. Remember, he will be watching you. He mustn't see you take the train for Etretat."

"I'll do my best," I said.

"And don't make mountains out of mole-hills. You see, you've been distrusting yourself needlessly. One mustn't be too timid!"

"Do you think I'm too timid?" I demanded, eager instantly to prove the contrary.

But she saw the light in my eyes, I suppose, for she drew away, almost imperceptibly.

"Only in some things," she retorted, and silenced me.

The evening passed and the last day came. We sighted land soon after breakfast—the high white cliffs of Cape La Hague—vague at first, but slowly lifting as we plowed on into the bay, with the crowded roofs of Havre far ahead.

I was standing at the rail beside Miss Kemball, filled with the thought of our imminent good-by, when she turned to me suddenly.

"Don't forget Martigny," she cautioned. "Wouldn't you better see him again?"

"I thought I'd wait till we landed," I said; "then I can help him off the boat and see him well away from the station. He's too ill to be very lively on his feet. We shouldn't have any trouble dodging him."

"Yes; and be careful. He mustn't suspect Etretat. But look at that clump of houses yonder—aren't they picturesque?"

They were picturesque, with their high red roofs and yellow gables and striped awnings; yet I didn't care to look at them. I was glad to perceive what a complicated business it was, getting our boat to the quay, for I was jealous of every minute; but it was finally accomplished in the explosive French manner, and after a further short delay the gang-plank was run out.

"And now," said my companion, holding out her hand, "we must say good-by."

"Indeed, not!" I protested. "See, there go your mother and Royce. They're evidently expecting us to follow. We'll have to help you with your baggage."

"Our baggage goes through to Paris—we make our declarations there."

"At least, I must take you to the train."

"You are risking everything!" she cried. "We can say good-by here as well as on the platform."

"I don't think so," I said.

"I have already said good-by to all my other friends!"

"But I refuse to be treated just like all the others," and I started with her down the gang-plank.

She looked at me from the corner of her eyes, her lips trembling between indignation and amusement.

"Do you know," she said deliberately, "I am beginning to fear that you are obstinate, and I abhor obstinate people."

"I'm not at all obstinate," I objected. "I'm simply contending for my rights."

"Your rights?"

"My right to be with you as long as I can, for one."

"Are there others?"

"Many others. Shall I enumerate them?"

"No," she said, "we haven't time. Here is mother."

They were to take the company's special train to Paris, which was waiting on the wharf, two hundred feet away, and we slowly pushed our way toward it. In the clamor and hurry and confusion wholly Latin, there was no chance for intelligent converse. The place was swarming with people, each of them, as it seemed to me, on the verge of hysteria. Someone, somewhere, was shouting "En voiture!" in a stentorian voice. Suddenly, we found our way blocked by a uniformed official, who demanded to see our tickets.

"You can't come any farther, I'm afraid," said Mrs. Kemball, turning to us. "We'll have to say good-by," and she held out her hand. "But we'll soon see you both again in Paris. You have the address?"

"Oh, yes!" I assured her; I felt that there was no danger of my ever forgetting it.

"Very well, then; we shall look for you," and she shook hands with both of us.

For an instant, I felt another little hand in mine, a pair of blue eyes smiled up at me in a way—

—

"Good-by, Mr. Lester," said a voice. "I shall be all impatience till we meet again."

"So shall I," and I brightened. "That was nice of you, Miss Kemball."

"Oh, I shall be anxious to hear how you succeeded," she retorted. "You will bring Miss Holladay to us?"

"If we find her, yes."

"Then, again, good-by."

She waved her hand, smiling, and was lost in the crowd.

"Come on, Lester," said Mr. Royce's voice. "There's no use standing staring here. We've got our own journey to look after," and he started back along the platform.

Then, suddenly, I remembered Martigny.

"I'll be back in a minute," I called, and ran up the gang-plank. "Has M. Martigny left the ship yet?" I inquired of the first steward I met.

"Martigny?" he repeated. "Martigny? Let me see."

"The sick gentleman in 375," I prompted.

"Oh, yes," he said. "I do not know, monsieur."

"Well, no matter. I'll find out myself."

I mounted to the upper deck, and knocked at the door of 375. There was no response. After a moment, I tried the door, but it was locked. The window, however, was partly open, and, shading my eyes with my hands, I peered inside. The stateroom was empty.

A kind of panic seized me as I turned away. Had he, indeed, seen through my artifice? In attempting to blind him, had I merely uncovered my own plan? Or—and my cheeks burned at the thought!—was he so well intrenched that he had no fear of me? Were his plans so well laid that it mattered not to him whither I went or what I did? After all, I had no assurance of success at Etretat—no proof that the fugitives had gone there—no reasonable grounds to believe that we should find them. Perhaps, indeed, Paris would be a better place to look for them; perhaps Martigny's advice had really been well meant.

I passed a moment of heart-rending uncertainty; I saw quite clearly what a little, little chance of success we had. But I shook the feeling off, sought the lower deck, and inquired again for Martigny. At last, the ship's doctor told me that he had seen the sick man safely to a carriage, and had heard him order the driver to proceed to the Hotel Continental.

"And, frankly, Mr. Lester," added the doctor, "I am glad to be so well rid of him. It is most fortunate that he did not die on the voyage. In my opinion, he is very near the end."

I turned away with a lighter heart. From a dying man there could not be much to fear. So I hunted up Mr. Royce, and found him, finally, endeavoring to extract some information from a supercilious official in a gold-laced uniform.

It was, it seemed, a somewhat complicated proceeding to get to Etretat. In half an hour, a train would leave for Beuzeville, where we must transfer to another line to Les Ifs; there a second transfer would be necessary before we could reach our destination. How long would it take? Our informant shrugged his shoulders with fine nonchalance. It was impossible to say. There had been a heavy storm two days before, which had blown down wires and damaged the little spur of track between Les Ifs and the sea. Trains were doubtless running again over the branch, but we could not, probably, reach Etretat before morning.

Amid this jumble of uncertainties, one definite fact remained—a train was to leave in half an hour, which we must take. So we hurried back to the boat, made our declaration, had our boxes examined perfunctorily and passed, bought our tickets, saw our baggage transferred, tipped a dozen people, more or less, and finally were shut into a compartment two minutes before the hour.

Then, in that first moment of inactivity, the fear of Martigny came back upon me. Had he really gone to the hotel? Had he deemed us not worth watching? Or had he watched? Was he on the train with us? Was he able to follow? The more I thought of him, the more I doubted my ability to deceive him.

I looked out cautiously from the window, up and down the platform, but saw no sign of him, and in a moment more we rattled slowly away over the switches. I sank back into my seat with a sigh of relief. Perhaps I had really blinded him!

An hour's run brought us to Beuzeville, where we were dumped out, together with our luggage, in a little frame station. An official informed us that we must wait there three hours for the train for Les Ifs. Beyond that? He could not say. We might possibly reach Etretat next day.

"How far is Les Ifs from here?" inquired my companion.

"About twelve kilometers, monsieur."

"And from there to Etretat?"

"Is twenty kilometers more, monsieur."

"Thirty-two kilometers altogether," said Mr. Royce. "That's about twenty miles. Why can't we drive, Lester? We ought to cover it easily in three hours—four at the most."

Certainly it seemed better than waiting on the uncertain railway, and we set at once about the work of finding a vehicle. I could be of little use, since English was an unknown tongue at Beuzeville, and even Mr. Royce's French was sorely taxed, but we succeeded at last in securing a horse and light trap, together with a driver who claimed to know the road. All this had taken time, and the sun was setting when we finally drove away northward.

The road was smooth and level—they manage their road-making better in France—and we bowled along at a good rate past cultivated fields with little dwellings like doll-houses dotted here and there. Occasionally we passed a man or woman trudging along the road, but as the darkness deepened, it became more and more deserted. In an hour and a half from Beuzeville we reached Les Ifs, and here we stopped for a light supper. We had cause to congratulate ourselves that we had secured a vehicle at Beuzeville, for we learned that no train would start for Etretat until morning. The damage wrought by the storm of two days before had not yet been repaired, the wires were still down, and we were warned that the road was badly washed in places.

Luckily for us, the moon soon arose, so that we got forward without much difficulty, though slowly; and an hour before midnight we pulled up triumphantly before the Hotel Blanquet, the principal inn of Etretat. We lost no time in getting to bed; for we wished to be up betimes in the morning, and I fell asleep with the comforting belief that we had at last eluded Monsieur Martigny.

## CHAPTER XVII: Etretat

We were up at an hour which astonished the little fat keeper of the inn, and inquired the location of the office of the registrar of births. It was two steps away in the Rue Alphonse Karr, but would not be open for three hours, at least. Would messieurs have their coffee now? No, messieurs would not have their coffee until they returned. Where would they find the residence of the registrar of births? His residence, that was another matter. His residence was some little distance away, near the Casino, at the right—we should ask for Maître Fingret—anyone could tell us. When should messieurs be expected to return? It was impossible to say.

We set off along the street, leaving the inn-keeper staring after us—along the Rue Alphonse Karr, lined on both sides by houses, each with its little shop on the ground floor. Three minutes' walk brought us to the bay, a pretty, even picturesque place, with its perpendicular cliffs and gayly-colored fishing-smacks. But we paused for only a glance at it, and turned toward the Casino at the other end. "Maître Fingret?" we inquired of the first passer-by, and he pointed us to a little house, half-hidden in vines.

A knock brought the notary himself to the door, a little dried-up man, with keen face, and eyes incredibly bright. My companion explained our errand in laborious French, supplemented by much gesticulation—it is wonderful how the hands can help one to talk!—and after a time the little Frenchman caught his meaning, and bustled away to get his hat and coat, scenting a fat fee. Our first step was to be an easy one, thanks to the severity and thoroughness of French administration, but I admit that I saw not what we should do further, once we had verified the date of Miss Holladay's birth. The next step must be left to chance.

The notary unlocked the door, showed us into his office, and set out chairs for us. Then he got down his register of births for 1876. It was not a large book, for the births at Etretat are not overwhelming in number.

"The name, I think you said, was Holladay?" he asked.

"Hiram W. Holladay," nodded Mr. Royce.

"And the date June 10th?"

"Yes—June 10th."

The little man ran his finger rapidly down the page, then went back again and read the entries one by one more slowly, with a pucker of perplexity about his lips. He turned the leaf, began farther back, and read through the list again, while we sat watching him. At last he shut the book with a little snap and looked up at us.

"Messieurs," he said quietly, "no such birth is recorded here. I have examined the record for the months of May, June, and July."

"But it must be there!" protested Mr. Royce.

"Nevertheless it is not here, monsieur."

"Could the child have been born here and no record made of it?"

"Impossible, monsieur. No physician in France would take that responsibility."

"For a large fee, perhaps," suggested my companion.

"In Paris that may, sometimes, be possible. But in a small place like this, I should have heard of it, and it would have been my duty to investigate."

"You have been here for that length of time, then?"

"Oh, yes, monsieur," smiled the little man. "For a much longer time than that."

Mr. Royce leaned forward toward him. He was getting back all his old power as a cross-examiner.

"Monsieur Fingret," he began impressively, "I am quite certain that Hiram W. Holladay and his wife were here during the months of May, June, and July, 1876, and that while they were here a daughter was born to them. Think again—have you no recollection of them or of the event?"

The little notary sat for some moments with knitted brows. At last he shook his head.

"That would be the height of the season, you see, monsieur," he said apologetically. "There are a great many people here, at that time, and I cannot know all of them. Nevertheless, it seemed to me for a moment that there was about the name a certain familiarity—as of an old tune, you know, forgotten for years. Yet it must have been my fancy merely, for I have no recollection of the event you mention. I cannot believe that such a birth took place at Etretat."

There was one other chance, and I gave Mr. Royce the clew.

"Monsieur Fingret," he asked, "are you acquainted with a man by the name of Pierre Bethune?"

And again the notary shook his head.

"Or Jasper Martigny?"

"I never before heard either name, monsieur," he answered.

We sat silent a moment, in despair. Was our trip to Etretat to be of no avail? Where was my premonition, now? If we had lost the trail thus early in the chase, what hope was there that we should ever run down the quarry? And how explain the fact that no record had been made of Frances Holladay's birth? Why should her parents have wished to conceal it? Would they not naturally have been anxious to see that it was properly recorded?

An hour had passed; the shops were opening, and a bustle of life reached us through the open door. People began to pass by twos and threes.

"The first train for three days is about to arrive," said the little notary. "You see, this is a very small town, messieurs. The arrival of a train is an event."

Again we fell silent. Mr. Royce got out his purse and paid the fee. We had come to an impasse—a closed way, we could go no farther. I could see that the notary was a-hungered for his roll and coffee. With a sigh, I arose to go. The notary stepped to the door and looked up the street.

"Ah," he said, "the train has arrived, but it seems there were not many passengers. Here is one, though, who has finished a long journey."

He nodded to someone who approached slowly, it seemed. He was before the door—he passed on—it was Martigny!

"That is the man!" I cried to Mr. Royce. "That is Martigny! Ask who he really is."

He understood on the instant, and caught the notary's arm.

"Monsieur Fingret, who is that man?"

The notary glanced at him, surprised by his vehemence.

"That," he said, "is Victor Fajolle. He is just home from America and seems very ill, poor fellow."

"And he lives here?"

"Oh, surely; on the cliffs just above the town—the first house—you cannot miss it—buried in a grove of trees. He married the daughter of Madame Alix some years ago—he was from Paris."

"And his wife is living?"

"Oh, surely, she is living; she herself returned from America but three weeks ago, together with her mother and sister. The sister, they say, is—well——" and he finished with a significant gesture toward his head.

I saw my companion's face turn white—I steadied myself with an effort. I knew that, at last, the veil was to be lifted.

"And they are at home now?"

"I believe so," said the notary, eying him with more and more astonishment. "They have been keeping close at home since their return—they will permit no one to see the—invalid. There has been much talk about it."

"Come, we must go!" I cried. "He must not get there before us!"

But a sudden light gleamed in the notary's eyes.

"Wait, messieurs!" he cried. "A moment. But a moment. Ah, I remember it now—it was the link which was wanting, and you have supplied it—Holladay, a millionaire of America, his wife, Madame Alix—she did not live in the villa, then, messieurs. Oh, no; she was very poor, a nurse—anything to make a little money; her husband, who was a fisherman, was drowned, and left her to take care of the children as best she could. Ah, I remember—one a mere baby!"

He had got down another book, and was running his finger rapidly down the page—his finger all a-tremble with excitement. Suddenly, he stopped with a little cry of triumph.

"Here it is, messieurs! I knew I could not be mistaken! See!"

Under the date of June 10, 1876, was an entry of which this is the English:

"Holladay, Hiram W., and Elizabeth, his wife, of the city of New York, United States of America; from Céleste Alix, widow of Auguste Alix, her daughter Céleste, aged five months. All claim surrendered in consideration of the payment of 25,000 francs."

Mr. Royce caught up the book and glanced at the back. It was the "Record of Adoptions."

## CHAPTER XVIII: The Veil is Lifted

In a moment we were hurrying along the street, in the direction the notary had pointed out to us. Martigny was already out of sight, and we had need of haste. My head was in a whirl. So Frances Holladay was not really the daughter of the dead millionaire! The thought compelled a complete readjustment of my point of view. Of course, she was legally his daughter; equally of course, this new development could make no difference in my companion's feeling for her. Nothing, then, was really changed. She must go back with us; she must take up the old life—— But I had no time to reason it all out.

We had reached the beach again, and we turned along it in the direction of the cliffs. Far ahead, I saw a man hurrying in the same direction—I could guess at what agony and danger to himself. The path began to ascend, and we panted up it to the grassy down, which seemed to stretch for miles and miles to the northward. Right before us was a little wood, in the midst of which I caught a glimpse of a farmhouse.

We ran toward it, through a gate, and up the path to the door. It was closed, but we heard from within a man's excited voice—a resonant voice which I knew well. I tried the door; it yielded, and we stepped into the hall. The voice came from the room at the right. It was no time for hesitation—we sprang to the door and entered.

Martigny was standing in the middle of the floor, fairly foaming at the mouth, shrieking out commands and imprecations at two women who cowered in the farther corner. The elder one I knew at a glance—the younger—my heart leaped as I looked at her—was it Miss Holladay? No, yet strangely like.

He saw their startled eyes turn past him to us, and swung sharply round. For an instant he stood poised like a serpent about to strike, then I saw his eyes fix in a frightful stare, his face turned livid, and with a strangled cry, he fell back and down. Together we lifted him to the low window-seat, pursuers and pursued alike, loosened his collar, chafed his hands, bathed his temples, did everything we could think of doing; but he lay there staring at the ceiling with clenched teeth. At last Royce bent and laid his ear against his breast. Then he arose and turned gently to the women.

"It is no use," he said. "He is dead."

I looked to see them wince under the blow; but they did not. The younger woman went slowly to the window and stood there sobbing quietly; the other's face lit up with a positive blaze of joy.

"So," she exclaimed, in that low, vibrant voice I so well remembered, "so he is dead! That treacherous, cruel heart has burst at last!"

Royce gazed at her a moment in astonishment. She looked not at him, but at the dead man on the window-seat, her hands clasping and unclasping.

"Madame Alix," he said, at last, "you know our errand—we must carry it out."

She bowed her head.

"I know it, monsieur," she answered. "But for him, there would have been no such errand. As it is, I will help you all I can. Cécile," she called to the woman at the window, "go and bring your sister to these gentlemen."

The younger woman dried her eyes and left the room. We waited in tense silence, our eyes on the door. We heard the sound of footsteps on the stair; a moment, and she was on the threshold.

She came in slowly, listlessly—it gave me a shock to see the pallor of her face. Then she glanced up and saw Royce standing there; she drew in her breath with a quick gasp, a great wave of color swept over her cheeks and brow, a great light sprang into her eyes.

"Oh, John!" she cried, and swayed toward him.

He had her in his arms, against his heart, and the glad tears sprang to my eyes as I looked at them. I glanced at the elder woman, and saw that her eyes were shining and her lips quivering.

"And I have come to take you away, my love," he was saying.

"Oh, yes; take me away," she sobbed, "before the other comes."

She stopped, her eyes on the window-seat, where "the other" lay, and the color died out of her cheeks again.

"He, at least, has paid the penalty," said Royce. "He can trouble you no more, my love."

She was sobbing helplessly upon his shoulder, but as the moments passed she grew more calm, and at last stood upright from him. The younger woman had come back into the room, and was watching her curiously, with no trace of emotion.

"Come, let us go," said the girl. "We must take the first boat home."

But Royce held back.

"There has been a crime committed," he said slowly. "We must see that it is punished."

"A crime? Oh, yes; but I forgive them, dear."

"The crime against yourself you may forgive; but there was another crime—murder——"

"There was no murder!" burst in Cécile Alix. "I swear it to you, monsieur. Do you understand? There was no murder!"

I saw Miss Holladay wince at the other's voice, and Royce saw it, too.

"I must get her to the inn," he said. "This is more than she can bear—I fear she will break down utterly. Do you stay and get the story, Lester. Then we'll decide what it is best to do."

He led her away, out of the house and down the path, not once looking back. I watched them till the trees hid them, and then turned to the women.

"Now," I said, "I shall be happy to hear the story."

"It was that man yonder who was the cause of it all," began the mother, clasping her hands tightly in her lap to keep them still. "Four years ago he came from Paris here to spend the summer—he was ver' ill—his heart. We had been living happily, my daughter and I, but for the one anxiety of her not marrying. He met her and proposed marriage. He was ver' good—he asked no dowry, and, besides, my daughter was twenty-five years old—past her first youth. But she attracted him, and they were married. He took her back to Paris, where he had a little theater, a hall of the dance—but he grew worse again, and came back here. It was then that he found out that I had another daughter, whom I had given to a rich American. I was ver' poor, monsieur," she added piteously. "My man had died——"

"Yes, madame, I know," I said, touched by her emotion. Plainly she was telling the truth.

"So he wrote to friends in Amérique, and made questions about Monsieur Holladay. He learned—oh, he learned that he was ver' rich—what you call a man of millions—and that his daughter—my daughter, monsieur—was living still. From that moment, he was like a man possessed. At once he formed his plan, building I know not what hopes upon it. He drilled us for two years in speaking the English; he took us for six months to Londres that we might better learn. Day after day we took our lessons there—always and always English. Cécile learned ver' well, monsieur; but I not so well, as you can see—I was too old. Then, at last we reached New York, and my daughter—this one—was sent to see Monsieur Holladay, while I was directed that I write to Céleste—to Mademoiselle Holladay. She came that ver' afternoon," she continued, "and I told her that it was I who was her mother. He was with me, and displayed to her the papers of adoption. She could not but be convinced. He talked to her as an angel—oh, he could seem one when he chose!—he told her that I was in poverty—he made her to weep, which was what he desired. She promised to bring us money; she was ver' good; my heart went out to her. Then, just as she had arisen to start homeward, in Céleste came, crying, sobbing, stained with blood."

She shuddered and clasped her hands before her eyes.

"But you have said it was not murder, madame," I said to the younger woman.

"Nor was it!" she cried. "Let me tell you, monsieur. I reached the great building, which my husband had already pointed out to me; I went up in the lift; I entered the office, but saw no one. I went on through an open door and saw an old man sitting at a desk. I inquired if Mr. Holladay was there. The old man glanced at me and bowed toward another door. I saw it was a private office and entered it. The door swung shut behind me. There was another old man sitting at a desk, sharpening a pencil."

"'Is it you, Frances?' he asked.

"'No,' I said, stepping before him. 'It is her sister, Monsieur Holladay!'

"He stared up at me with such a look of dismay and anger on his face that I was fairly frightened; then, in the same instant, before I could draw breath, before I could say another word, his face grew purple, monsieur, and he fell forward on his desk, on his hand, on the knife, which was clasped in it. I tried to check the blood, but could not, it poured forth in such a stream. I knew not what to do; I was distracted, and in a frenzy, I left the place and hurried to our lodgings. That is the truth, monsieur; believe me."

"I do believe you," I said; and she turned again to the window to hide her tears.

"It was then," went on her mother, "that that man yonder had another inspiration. Before it had been only—what you call—blackmail—a few thousands, perhaps a pension; now it was something more—he was playing for a greater stake. I do not know all that he planned. He found Céleste suspected of having killed her father; he must get her released at any cost; so he wrote a note——"

"Yes," I cried. "Yes, of course; I see. Miss Holladay under arrest was beyond his reach."

"Yes," she nodded, "so he wrote a note—oh, you should have seen him in those days! He was like some furious wild beast. But after she was set free, Céleste did not come to us as she had promise'. We saw that she suspected us, that she wish' to have nothing more to do with us; so

Victor commanded that I write another letter, imploring her, offering to explain." She stopped a moment to control herself. "Ah, when I think of it! She came, monsieur. We took from her her gown and put it on Cécile. She never left the place again until the carriage stopped to take her to the boat. As for us—we were his slaves—he guided each step—he seemed to think of everything—to be prepared for everything—he planned and planned."

There was no need that she should tell me more—the whole plot lay bare before me—simple enough, now that I understood it, and carried out with what consummate finish!

"One thing more," I said. "The gold."

She drew a key from her pocket and gave it to me.

"It is in a box upstairs," she said. "This is the key. We have not touched it."

I took the key and followed her to the floor above. The box, of heavy oak bound with iron, with steamship and express labels fresh upon it, stood in one corner. I unlocked it and threw back the lid. Package upon package lay in it, just as they had come from the sub-treasury. I locked the box again, and put the key in my pocket.

"Of course," I said, as I turned to go, "I can only repeat your story to my companion. He and Miss Holladay will decide what steps to take. But I am sure they will be merciful."

They bowed without replying, and I went out along the path between the trees, leaving them alone with their dead.

And it was of the dead I thought last and most sorrowfully: a man of character, of force, of fascination. How I could have liked him!

## CHAPTER XIX: The End of the Story

Paris in June! Do you know it, with its bright days and its soft nights, murmurous with voices? Paris with its crowded pavements—and such a crowd, where every man and woman awakens interest, excites speculation! Paris, with its blue sky and its trees, and its color—and its fascination there is no describing!

Joy is a great restorer, and a week of happiness in this enchanted city had wrought wonders in our junior and his betrothed. It was good to look at them—to smile at them sometimes; as when they stood unseeing before some splendid canvas at the Louvre. The past was put aside, forgotten; they lived only for the future.

And a near future, too. There was no reason why it should be deferred; we had all agreed that they were better married at once; so, that decided, the women sent us about our own affairs, and spent the intervening fortnight in a riot of visits to the costumer: for, in Paris, even for a very quiet wedding, a bride must have her trousseau. But the great day came at last; the red tape of French administration was successfully unknotted; and at noon they were wedded, with only we three for witnesses, at the pretty chapel of St. Luke's, near the Boulevard Montparnasse.

There was a little breakfast afterward at Mrs. Kemball's apartment, and then our hostess bade them adieu, and her daughter and I drove with them across Paris to the Gare de Lyon, where they were to take train for a fortnight on the Riviera. We waved them off and turned back together.

"It is a desecration to use a carriage on such a day," said my companion: so we dismissed ours and sauntered afoot down the Boulevard Diderot toward the river.

"So that is the end of the story," she said musingly.

"Of their story, yes," I interjected.

"But there are still certain things I do not quite understand," she continued, not heeding me. "Yes?"

"For instance—why did they trouble to keep her prisoner?"

"Family affection?"

"Nonsense! There could be none. Besides the man dominated them; and I believe him to have been capable of any crime."

"Perhaps he meant the hundred thousand to be only the first payment. With her at hand, he might hope to get more indefinitely. Without her——"

"Well, without her?"

"Oh, the plot grows and grows, the more one thinks of it! I believe it grew under his hands in just the same way. I don't doubt that it would have come, at last, to Miss Holladay's death by some subtle means; to the substitution of her sister for her—after a year or two abroad, who could have detected it? And then—oh, then, she would have married Fajolle again, and they would have settled down to the enjoyment of her fortune. And he would have been a great man—oh, a very great man. He would have climbed and climbed."

My companion nodded.

"Touché!" she cried.

I bowed my thanks; I was learning French as rapidly as circumstances permitted.

"But Frances did not see them again?"

"Oh, no; she preferred not."

"And the money?"

"Was left in the box. I sent back the key. She wished it so. After all, it was her mother——"

"Yes, of course; perhaps she was not really so bad."

"She wasn't," I said decidedly. "But the man——"

"Was a genius. I'm almost sorry he's dead."

"I'm more than sorry—it has taken an interest out of life."

We had come out upon the bridge of Austerlitz, and paused, involuntarily. Below us was the busy river, with its bridges, its boats, its crowds along the quays; far ahead, dominating the scene, the towers of the cathedral; and the warm sun of June was over it all. We leaned upon the balustrade and gazed at all this beauty.

"And now the mystery is cleared away," she said, "and the prince and the princess are wedded, just as they were in the fairy tales of our childhood. It's a good ending."

"For all stories," I added.

She turned and looked at me.

"There are other stories," I explained. "Theirs is not the only one."

"No?"

The spirit of Paris—or perhaps the June sunshine—was in my veins, running riot, clamorous, not to be repressed.

"Certainly not. There might be another, for instance, with you and me as the principals."

I dared not look at her; I could only stare ahead of me down at the water.

She made no sign; the moments passed.

"Might be," I said desperately. "But there's a wide abyss between the possible and the actual."

Still no sign; I had offended her—I might have known!

But I mustered courage to steal a sidelong glance at her.

She was smiling down at the water, and her eyes were very bright.

"Not always," she whispered. "Not always."

Transcriber's notes:

Variations in spelling have been left as in the original.

The following changes have been made to the text:

Page 33: "possibilty" corrected to "possibility" ("... precluding the possibility of anyone swinging down from above ...")

Page 183: "Cafe" corrected to "Café" ("At the Café Jourdain")

Page 268: "sat" corrected to "set" ("... and we set at once about the work of finding a vehicle.")

Page 280: erroneous chapter numbering corrected, for the chapter title "The Veil is Lifted" ("Chapter XVII" corrected to "Chapter XVIII")

Made in the USA
Monee, IL
21 November 2023